HIGH QUEEN

Book Two of the Ulfr Crisis

BADELGARD, THE COUNTRY OF THE NORTHMEN

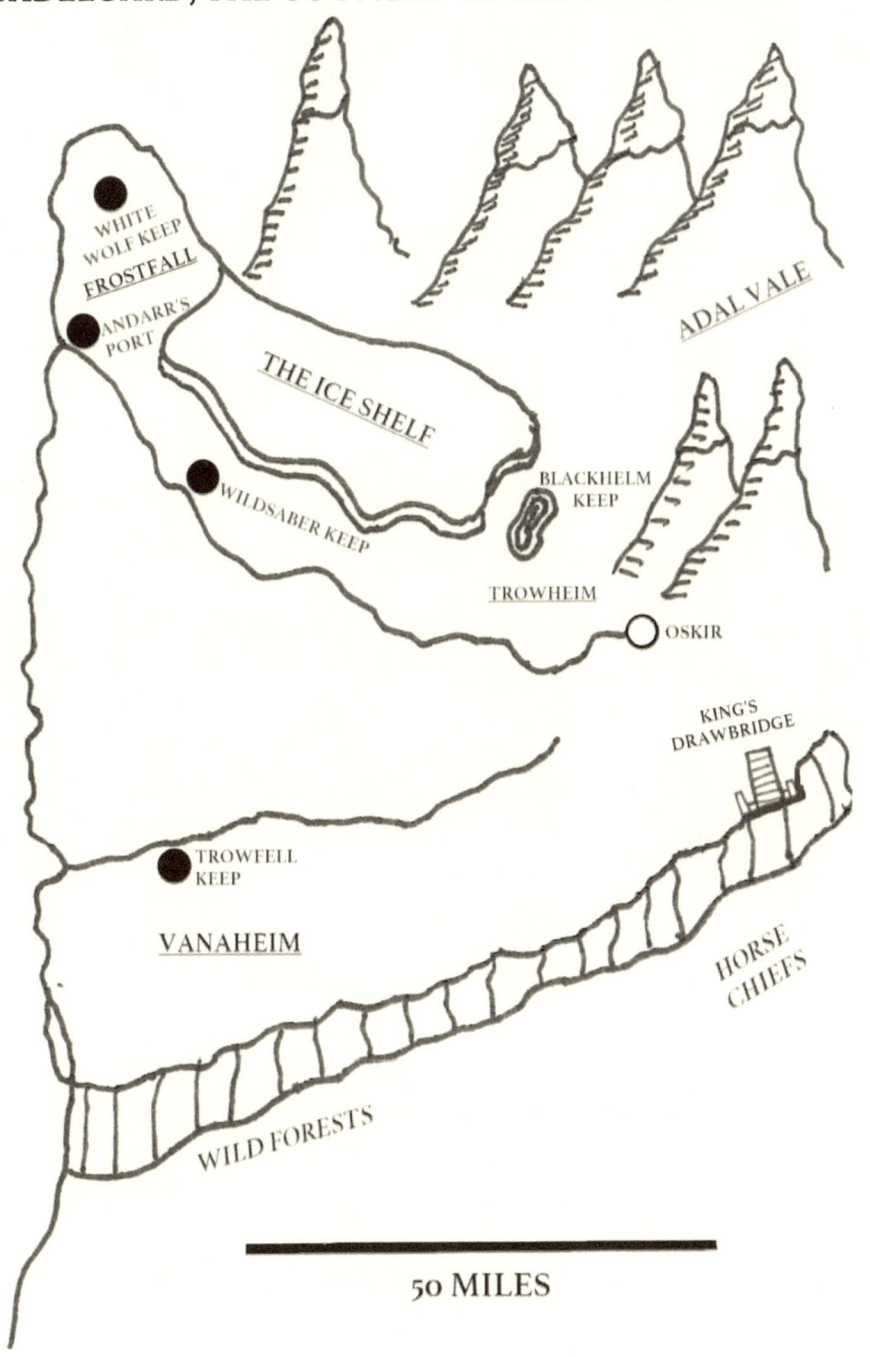

WHITE WOLF KEEP

FROSTFALL

ANDARR'S PORT

ADAL VALE

THE ICE SHELF

WILDSABER KEEP

BLACKHELM KEEP

TROWHEIM

OSKIR

KING'S DRAWBRIDGE

TROWFELL KEEP

VANAHEIM

HORSE CHIEFS

WILD FORESTS

50 MILES

Table of Contents

CHAPTER ONE:
KAI RIVERHALL

The little girl stumbled toward Kai Riverhall, her eyes glassy and frozen, her lips rimmed with dried blood. She was a darkling, but even battle-hardened Kai found it difficult to strike down someone who was—or once had been—so young.

"Don't kill me," she whispered without moving her lips. "Please?"

Kai gulped.

"Stay still," said the darkling girl. "Just… let me touch you."

Kai released the bowstring. The arrow flew forward and pierced her icy, frozen forehead. She shrieked and fell to the ground. Darklings could only be killed via a blow to the head. Sword, club, arrow—it didn't matter what weapon, as long as you hit in the right spot.

This was Kai's first kill of the day, but it almost certainly would not be his last. The darklings wandered the forest in increasing numbers. Scoutmaster Frey wanted every one of his underlings to kill at least ten daily. Lately, the darklings hadn't retreated into shadows at day; it seemed they were now immune to the rays of the sun.

Kai walked up to the corpse and stooped down. The girl wore a soft white dress—silk, it looked like. Once, she was a rich girl; perhaps even related to the Riverhalls.

Kai was a Riverhall too. Ha! He had no silk clothing. Being a Riverhall did not mean that you were rich, at least not in the Order of Scouts. He drew back his hand before he could touch her skin.

Do not touch the darklings, Frey had said. *Do not touch them, or anything they carry.*

Kai wandered through the forest, silent as a lynx, waiting for a darkling to pop out at any moment. One of them had wounded his fellow scout, Uthrik; Scoutmaster Frey had to decapitate him with a sword. Kai did not want to repeat Uthrik's fate.

Rustling began above, up a steep ridge. Kai backed away and fitted an arrow to his string. There was something in the leafy green up above—a presence that made Kai's neck-hairs stand on end and a chill pass through his body.

Something grunted. Then, rustling began in the ferns. Heavy, trudging footsteps echoed through the air. The gait of the creature—whoever it was—was slow and confused. It had two feet—Kai could tell that much—and it was not a deer or a lynx. Could it be a bear? The footsteps certainly sounded heavy enough.

A lump grew in Kai's throat. "Who are you?" he whimpered.

"*Sio Soreldi*," a voice said.

Kai gulped. "Pardon?"

"*Cani Orion. Miuru.*"

The scent of rot, earth, and the juices of the grave filled Kai's nostrils. He looked up at the cliff inquisitively. The creature was close now.

Kai shuddered and his fingers trembled. The arrow loosed of its own accord. It soared through the air and hit a tree. Kai thought of running. The creature's footsteps indicated it was close, now.

He looked up at the cliff. What came next, he didn't remember.

The triangular pinewood ceiling of Woodhome stretched above him, and the burning logs of a hearth-fire bathed him in light. The moose heads and deer heads hung along the log walls. Kai was at home.

"He's not moving," said the voice of Scoutmaster Frey. The man's long golden hair dangled below his shoulders. His brown eyes scanned up and down Kai's body.

"I found him in the Ninth Ward," said Helgun, Kai's best friend, as he stepped into view.

Frey ran his coarse woodsman's fingers across Kai's arms. "Do you remember what happened? What did you see?"

Kai described what he had heard. He described the terror he had felt, but he remembered nothing more. "Looking back, I think I sensed a creeping power from him. Some kind of aura, but it was dark… evil…"

"You remember nothing," Frey said. "What you did see you have forgotten. Witchcraft, indeed."

Kai turned his head and looked around. Everything stood in its proper place: the orange log walls, the brown bearskin rugs, and the antlered heads of stags on the walls. Yet he did not feel altogether well. "I wonder if I'll ever remember what happened."

"Trust and believe," said Master Frey. "Then, perhaps."

"He told me '*Sio Soreldi*' and '*Cani Orion. M——*'"

Frey hushed him. "Stay your tongue," he snapped. "Do not speak the language of the Ulfr."

Kai raised a brow. "The words are in the Ulfr language?"

"They sound like it."

"If it is the Ulfr tongue, we can send for a lexicon," Kai answered. "We can go to Oskir——"

"The king will not let us borrow such a valuable book," Master Frey answered. "You know this as well as I. Besides, Oskir is far… "

"We can go to the library ourselves," Kai said. "Surely the darklings have no interest in books or learning."

"I will hear no more of it," Frey dismissed him. "Now relax the rest of the night." He walked away into the distance.

Kai tried to ease himself off the table. His muscles were tight, as stiff as the statues of Riverhall Forest. After a struggle he got moving again.

The next day, just as always, Kai went out on patrol. His muscles ached, and a headache clouded all thought. The fact that Frey assigned him the Twelfth Ward only partially explained his pains. The Twelfth

Ward comprised the north-eastern section of the Great Wood that bordered the ghost town of Andarr's Port. Though it used to be the safest, now the scouts dreaded patrolling it.

Despite the aches, he continued on and tried his best to hide his discomfort. The Scouts of Woodhome valued bravery, overcoming pain, and manliness above all other virtues. Harald, the baron and Kai's distant relation, did not believe in such virtues; and the Order of Scouts found it difficult to respect him.

An entire darkling family came into view: a man, a woman, and three toddling children. Their curse had turned their skin a pale, frosty hue and their eyes hard as icicles. Kai loosed five arrows in quick sequence and struck each one in the head. These were the slow darklings, the "shamblers." The living dead varied in strength, with shamblers as the weakest.

At about noon, Kai's wanderings took him to the edge of Andarr's Port. The sheer silence never failed to surprise him. In the past, when Kai patrolled the Twelfth Ward, the city's noise overwhelmed his senses. Now, on this cool summer day, the only sounds were the pitter-patter of rain and the wind howling through the empty buildings.

A shrill, panicked scream resounded through the air: a woman's scream.

Darklings don't sound like that.

He followed the scream to its source and found a woman—a rich woman, judging by her scarlet-dyed satin dress and jeweled golden necklaces. A large white stallion nickered nervously a few feet away.

A darkling crouched before the woman, fangs bared and claws extended. It had no right arm; only a frozen stump remained. Kai quietly circled the darkling, not wanting to scare it into attacking the woman. But he needed to shoot from a less dangerous angle.

At last, he pulled back his bow and released the bowstring. In an instant the arrow was through the darkling's head, and the monster fell to the ground.

The woman seemed more shocked at the explosion than grateful to Kai. Still, Kai made his way over to her. He trod slowly, making sure not to frighten her further.

"Milady?" Kai said in as gentlemanly a tone as he could muster.

"I heard the rumors about Andarr's Port, that it is a ghost town," the woman said, her brown eyes looking away from Kai as if he wasn't there. "I didn't think the darklings came out by day."

"Their power has grown, milady," Kai said. "Perhaps you should head east for safety."

"I am looking for my son," the woman said. "He has turned into one of *them*, but I know that if he looks into his mother's eyes, he will change back to normal."

"I advise against that, milady," Kai said. "The darklings cannot change back. Not even a mother's love can change them back."

"Do not call me a fool!" the woman snapped. "What is your station, boy?"

"I am highborn," Kai answered. "I am a Riverhall."

"Harald Riverhall is dead, and his wife Alysse has been exiled, never to return," the woman said. "The Line of Riverhall is vanquished. Only my son—the one I must reclaim—is a Riverhall. He is the last male Riverhall alive, but I, Kenna, will make him a proper Wildsaber."

Impossible. Kai looked at her closely. Her eyes seemed truthful. "What is a proper lady doing without a full guard?"

"They were eaten—" Kenna stopped whatever she was about to say. "I do not need to speak to you, Riverhall. I must find my son"

"Your son is gone, milady. He is not coming back."

"You don't know that," Kenna hissed. "My poor Stenn *will* come back to me. And I will find him."

"Suit yourself," Kai said, then turned and headed back toward the center of the forest—the First Ward, where Woodhome lay—to tell Scoutmaster Frey of the demise of Lord Harald and Lady Alysse.

CHAPTER TWO:
ALYSSE RIVERHALL

Things had not changed much in the kingdom of Zarubain. That was Alysse's first impression as she stepped off the riverboat and entered her father's land, the duchy of Voraigne. The boughs of the hemlocks and firs dripped with recent rain. Despite the wetness, warmth permeated the air. Alysse was warmer than she'd been in decades and for a brief second she wondered whether she might never return to Badelgard, but she cast that thought aside immediately. Her desire to set things right by far outweighed her desire for comfort.

Her father, Ergould Vis Voraigne, lived in a vast manor on a quiet lake. Vast compared to Riverhall Castle; not 'vast' compared to the manors of other dukes. It was not built specifically for comfort like Riverhall Castle; Voraigne Manor had tall stone walls, battlements, a moat, and a drawbridge. War between the kings' subjects was common in Zarubain, more common than it was in Badelgard; at least, more common than it currently was in Badelgard. Gods knew the earls used to fight with equal ferocity until the Oster dynasty came into control.

Jays, river thrushes and robins flitted through the moist evergreen forest, singing their beautiful songs. In Zarubain, Alysse had been taught that invisible fairies lived under the ponds and in the weeds and on the boughs of the trees, but she never believed it. Her father's fairy-priestess never impressed Alysse with her intelligence, even though Madame Flourelle had been taught at the Lady's Cathedral in Zarubad.

The manor appeared in view, a towering castle of dark gray against the almost-blinding greenness of the forest. It felt so strange to come back after so many years. What awaited her here? What had happened to her father, the honorable duke Ergould? Most importantly, what had happened to the House Vis Voraigne?

She crossed the distance to the castle. Mallards swam in the family lake. Paddling through the lily-covered water on a rowboat was her father. Age had turned his hair gray and his skin wrinkled. He still wore nice clothing: a fine purple tunic and woolen breeches, so very unlike the thick kirtles of Badelgard. Gold rings gleamed on his fingers and a glittering diamond brooch held his cloak together.

"Father!" Alysse cried, dropping her luggage.

Her father looked up at her. "My dear," he said, and began paddling toward her. Eventually he reached the shore and hauled himself onto the moist forest floor, each step obviously painful. "My dear Alysse... I was sure that I would never see you again."

"Father," she said, "it is so good to see you."

They embraced. "Alysse vis Voraigne," he said.

"Alysse Riverhall," she corrected him. "I will never change my name. I love Harald so, even though he is dead."

"Surely not!" Ergould cried. "He is too young to die. Was it illness?"

"He died in war, father," Alysse said. "The king of Badelgard murdered him. Then I was exiled."

Ergould gasped. "Those smelly, barbaric northmen! How dare they treat a woman of Vis Voraigne stock like that? It is criminal, I tell you... criminal! But now you can come back; live with me, and when your younger brother inherits the duchy you will live the rest of your life in comfort. It is not so bad."

"Father," Alysse said, "I have lived away from home too long. I have lived under Harald's protection too long. I am a daughter of Badelgard now..."

"Nonsense," said Ergould. "Our fortunes are increased. We own twice the land than when you left. Besides... once you have Zarube cuisine tonight, you won't be able to leave."

The fried snails, the sour crab roasts, the cheese-stuffed duckling and the fermented cow tongues brought memories back to Alysse, but that was all they did. Too long had Alysse feasted on the mead, the roast pork and the crispy potatoes of Badelgard. She no longer preferred the high cuisine of the Zarube king's court. In fact, it tasted strange to her, though she'd never tell her father that; insulting the king's culinary preferences was social suicide.

Her father devoured the fermented cow tongues, one after another. He had grown slightly plumper since Alysse had last seen him; nothing to worry about, but it was easy to see that he had chosen the relaxed life in his old age.

"Where is my brother?" Alysse said, glancing at a plate of butter-fried lamb eyes in distaste.

"Your brother Lourges is at war," said Ergould. "He has taken an army south into a petty count's lands and will be back by week's end. The duchy is expanding at a lynx's pace… and one day, even the Golden Lion of the king will not be able to stand against the Red Hawk."

For some reason, Alysse doubted that the king's standard would ever fall to the Vis Voraignes. "My dear father—one who gave me life—I must be honest with you. I need knights. I need soldiers. I need an army to take back Badelgard."

"Why does a woman need an army?" Ergould said.

"Not even in Zarubain—not even in the bloody *southlands*—can I escape woman-hatred!" Alysse glared at her father.

"I apologize, my dear," Ergould said. "I should not speak like one of the northmen. I simply do not understand why you won't stay here."

"I desire to return to my adopted home," Alysse said. "It has become a part of me, like an arm or a leg."

"Then we must cut it off," Ergould said. "The living in Zarubain is good. Wealth is plentiful, save for the dirty peasants. And the food—"

"I hate the food!" Alysse snapped. She had finally gathered the gumption. "I am sick of lamb's eyes, and boiled snail, and fermented cabbage. Don't you understand, father? I want an army more than anything. I need it."

"You cannot just come here, ask for an army, and leave!" Ergould said. "Think of your father! Think of your old, sickly father who has been so worried about his daughter. You have never written to me, Alysse. And now you show up in my twilight years and ask for an army."

"Father, I love you; and that's why you must do this," Alysse said.

Her statement contained a grain of truth. In some ways, she did love her father. In others she did not. He had sent her off at the age of fourteen to be married to a blasted northman. He hadn't listened to her tears as she begged him to let her stay home. He had told her, "You must do this for the sake of our line!" and "Have some respect for your family!" and finally, "I don't care about what you want!" That was why she hadn't written to him. Because Alysse held grudges. She held one of the biggest against her father because—even though Harald had turned out to be a good man and not much older than her—Ergould hadn't cared about what she wanted.

She did love her distant, uncaring father in some ways, because it was every daughter's duty to love her father if he did not abuse her. And Ergould hadn't abused her in any obvious way; only ignored her feelings, wants, and desires. Only ignored her. Only used her as a political tool.

"My daughter, you look angry," Ergould said. "I am sorry if I have offended you."

"No, you haven't," Alysse said. She reached out and touched his wrinkled old hand. "And if I was, I wasn't for long. I just wish you'd understand... I need to go back to Badelgard. A woman has slighted me... killed my husband... killed my dear friend and musician. Surely you can understand my wrath."

Ergould's expression softened. "I can," he said.

The rain picked up again in the evening. It was a cooling, misty rain. Alysse sat in her old bed with its feather-stuffed mattress and its purple drapes and looked outside the window into the yard, into the forest of firs and hemlocks. It was the ducal wood, set aside for the Master of the House Vis Voraigne. Just a mile away, the peasants' farms began.

The lowborn did not fare well in Badelgard, but in Zarubain they fared even worse. How many times, as a girl, had Alysse seen their wretchedness: their filthy hovels; their backbreaking work; their mangy, thin forms? And how much had Alysse taken for granted her high and lofty position, her life of comfort and plentiful food? It was not the duty of a noble to have pity on the poor, but Alysse felt for them anyway. They were pitiful and wretched, but they were people too; only people that had no luck.

She looked out the forest once again—a brilliantly green scene of moss-draped evergreens. She wondered if her brother would ever come back for war.

He did come back one stormy night, a week later. Outside, lightning flashed and thunder rolled through the ducal wood. At first, when there was a loud knocking on the door, Alysse thought it was just a series of harsh lightning-bolts. But her father got up from the table— they were having an unfortunate dinner of bread and duck-liver pate— and Alysse followed.

The door swung open before they reached it. A shadowy figure stood in the open doorway, dressed in a knee-length hauberk. He was pale and looked deathly tired. Alysse had never seen him as an adult, only as a child; when Alysse left at age fourteen, Lourges was only seven.

And what a tall, handsome man he had become, despite the effects of his obvious fatigue. His eyes were green like Alysse; he had an even face, a prominent jaw, and a button nose; and topping it all was a thick set of blond hair, held up by a headband.

"My brother!" Alysse cried.

"My sister," Lourges said, somewhat less emphatically. "I have not seen you for an age. If only you could see me in victory, and not in defeat."

"What do you mean?" Ergould said in an accusatory tone.

"The count of Garrone has routed our troops. He is a brilliant general, my father. I have disappointed you and brought shame to our noble house."

"How many men?" Ergould growled.

"Pardon?" Lourges said.

"*How many men?*" Ergould hissed.

"Two hundred common footmen have been killed. Sir Arcibaud, Sir Jierreau and Sir Jacouie have died and gone to see the gods, but fifty proper knights remain," Lourges said. "In all, it was not a bad loss; but any loss is a shame."

"It is a crime against nature for the House Vis Voraigne to lose against *anyone!*" Ergould shouted.

"I am sorry, father," Lourges said.

"Who commanded the retreat?" Ergould said. "If you still had some seven thousand footmen left, why did you not keep fighting?"

Indeed, Alysse thought. *Only a coward would retreat with those numbers.*

"Well," Lourges said, obviously not wanting to tell the truth. "The army was large, and Sir Jourmande—"

"Sir Jourmande is *not* the commanding field-marshal," Ergould said. "You are the leader of my army."

"They will not listen to me... they only listen to Sir Jourmande."

Then you are an even greater coward than I believed, Alysse thought.

"You are a wretch," Ergould said. "Now come and have some duck-liver pate. Actually, forget it; you may only eat bread as punishment."

Lourges' embarrassment was great, but the conversation

eventually turned to gentler topics. He asked if Alysse was with child.

"I am. My husband has died," Alysse said, and then, knowing she had to lie about the proper paternity, added, "But Harald has left me with a gift. A child is inside me, waiting to be born."

Lourges smiled weakly, despite the obvious shame written on his features. "If only he is half as strong as you... and as beautiful. Perhaps he will be."

"I am neither strong, nor am I particularly beautiful," Alysse said. "But thank you, brother." She forced down a bite of pate-smeared bread and washed it down with wine—a drink she only rarely enjoyed in Badelgard. She hesitated a second, wondering it was the proper time, and then finally spoke her mind. "These petty wars are not worth the army Vis Voraigne."

"How do you mean, sister?" said Lourges.

"The land of Badelgard is there for the taking," Alysse continued, carefully measuring the expression on Lourges' face and adjusting her tone properly. "With my help—as a Riverhall who is a legitimate contender to the throne by marriage—you could annex the land, and Badelgard could belong to our noble house."

Lourges laughed. "The northmen are smelly, dirty, and poor... barbarians at their cores. What interest would I have in them?"

"There is plentiful wealth there," Alysse said. "Iron mines, copper mines... furs, antlers, and endless timber... men and women fit—nay, *happy*—at the prospect of servitude." Alysse hated lying, but it was necessary. No Badelgard lowborn would happily enter into Zarube-style servitude.

"Pray tell, sister," Lourges said, "why you are here and not in Andarr's Port with your family?"

"The family is dead. Harald is dead. My skald is dead. A she-wolf, Lady Kenna, has slain them all." Alysse's cheeks grew flushed with anger. "Tell me, brother, how many men are under your command?"

"My dear sister," Lourges said, his voice dripping with derision, "I cannot agree to come with you and fight under the Riverhall banner.

Your request is foolish, and borders on childlike. Have I not mentioned our house is in peril?"

Alysse's anger diverted from Lady Kenna and focused on her brother. "It is only in peril because you are a cowa—" She caught herself. "—because your friend made a command to retreat."

"Do not talk to me in such a manner, sister," Lourges said. "You have asked for an answer and I have given it: a firm, resounding 'No.' If you intend to go back to Badelgard, you came here for naught. Your husband has died, and now you must return to our home—under your father's care, under my care."

"I will not be resigned to a prison," Alysse said. "I am free to make my own decisions and you have no say in them."

"Suit yourself," Lourges said, and a dark smile crept over his features. "But you won't be getting an army."

Alysse would see about that. Her brother lacked the courage and manhood to command his own troops; and Alysse was not discouraged easily.

CHAPTER THREE:
ERIK TROWFELL

Trowfell Keep and Vanaheim might be among the poorest places in the nation, but they had the Healing House. People from all over the country—north, south, east and west—came to experience its hot springs, its mud baths, its priests and physicians. So, too, did the Trowfells oversee the Temple of Vana on the edge of the Sky Cliffs. Prominent earls and barons sent their daughters to be trained under Headmistress Freya.

The derision—the cold stares, the ignored remarks—that the Trowfells experienced on their visits to Earls' Court was completely unjustified in Erik's mind. Even baronial families—those whom, with the exception of the Riverhalls, owned no great amount of land—treated his parents with disrespect. It was baffling.

Erik was writing a letter to some long-lost relation in White Wolf Keep. The inkwell had run dry, as it always did at the most inopportune moments.

He got up to replace it, leaving his room which—earls, take note!—had stone walls.

He reached the throne room. His mother Carolyn sat there, wearing the fur-lined winter cloak she never before wore in the summer. She chatted with a man in a green hood—in all likelihood, one of the rangers from whom she extracted gossip. Erik waited in the shadows a while, and then, when the excited gasps of his mother and the low murmuring of the ranger stopped, he presented himself.

As the man turned to leave, Erik said, "I have run out of ink."

"There is no ink," she responded. "That stuff is expensive, you know."

"It's important."

"There are more important things to worry about than writing letters to scheming peasants."

"He's not a peasant!"

"I have serious doubts about the bloodline of Sven 'Trufell'—if that really is his name." His mother laughed. "Besides, dark tidings have already reached my ears, and those are more important than ink."

"What do you mean?"

"The High King is dead. Alysse Riverhall has been exiled. Harald Riverhall—blessed Harald—was killed, and dozens more executed, lowborn and high. Sigmund Blackhelm believes he is the rightful king and will do anything to keep sitting upon the High Throne."

"The Osters have had the throne for ages!" Erik said incredulously. Indeed, the news was difficult to believe. "Surely the other houses have risen up…"

Carolyn shook her head. "The heads of the other houses only care about themselves. Hasn't life taught you such a lesson? They scheme and plot, caring nothing of honor. They are nothing like their Warden ancestors."

"Except us! We still believe in honor," Erik said. "We must do something about this. We must gather an army of our own. And yet… we must be careful, or it will all go to waste."

That night, Erik etched his plans on a wax tablet—the wax tablet that he had used with his writing tutors so many years ago. Sigmund Blackhelm likely had soldiers numbering in the tens of thousands, and all were well trained. To levy a lowborn army vast enough to match it, the number would have to be impossibly high.

"Erik." His mother stood at the doorway. "I have an idea of what we could do."

"What?"

"Do you remember Greta Oster?"

"Yes." Greta Oster, aunt to the former king, was a shrewd, high-strung, and honorable-to-the-death matron. She was an Oster through-and-through, a stern believer in their right to rule, and doubtlessly angered by the recent turn of events.

"She lives in Sky Hold in Somergard," Carolyn said. "She has an elite guard that could stand against a thousand of Sigmund's men. She would be a great ally."

Erik smiled. His mother was probably excited about her idea, poor thing. "Why would a woman of such stature march under the Trowfell banner?"

"She would not march under our banner," Carolyn said. "We would march under hers."

Erik frowned. "She is a widow, you know. She does not have a husband to lead the elite guard against Sigmund."

"I tend to the earldom's affairs in your father's absence. And besides… it does not matter if an army is led by a woman, a man, or a little boy when the enemy is at the end of a sword."

"Will you have me ride to Sky Hold?"

Carolyn nodded. "It is worth a try."

Erik started his journey at dawn. He made the fifty-mile distance in a single day, riding hard across the moss-lands and the pine-lands in the pelting rain and taking few breaks. In mid-afternoon, he reached Sky Hold: a plain stone castle that, in its own way, was remarkable. What made the hold remarkable was its position; it jutted partially off the Sky Cliffs in the face of the sheer two-thousand foot drop. Erik had heard many stories of the death sentences that Greta issued, and the manner in which the sentences were taken out. A stone platform jutted out into the open air, and gods help the rebel who feared heights.

A hostler took Erik's horse into the stables. Outside the gates of Sky Hold was a contingent of elite guards dressed in the red-gold of the Osters. Perhaps fifty of them stood watch outside the entryway; four-hundred more doubtlessly patrolled the grounds or stood within.

Erik shook some of the rain off his cloak. He passed through the wooden double-doors and entered the common room where, upon a raised dais and a wooden throne, sat Greta Oster. A silver tiara—the sign of an unlanded or marginally-landed noble—rested on her head of dark-gray hair. Her green eyes were shrewd and calculating; Erik did not want to ever face those eyes as an enemy.

"Greetings, Your Honor," he said, still shivering from the cold. He dropped to his knees. He waited until her command, to prove he was aware of his inferior status.

"Rise," Greta said sharply. "Erik Trowfell, son of Magnus and Carolyn Trowfell. You are young."

"I have seen seventeen winters, milady," Erik said. "Eighteen, if you count this summer as a winter."

The meager attempt at humor did not put a smile on Greta's face. Frowning, she said, "Speak your mind, Trowfell. You are welcome here."

"You are an honorable woman, Greta, and that is why I have come." Suddenly anxiety filled him—the gravity of what he was about to say didn't strike him when he was riding. "Sigmund Blackhelm, dare I say it, is not honorable."

Greta's cold gaze continued. "If you, Erik Trowfell, think that this sycophancy... this self-serving humility... this toadying ploy will work—"

Erik gulped and looked down. He wondered what it would be like when he was thrown off the Sky Cliffs.

"—then you are right. I hate Sigmund Blackhelm. I believe in the Osters' rule. I believe we should change our house's adage to 'Always the Osters!'"

"And the Trowfells would gladly adopt it as their battle-cry," Erik answered. "My mother is a supporter of Oster rule. We wish to pledge our armies to the Osters. I speak on behalf of my mother, Carolyn Oster, who rules in my father Henrik's absence."

Something like a smile touched Greta's face, but the ancient

Oster matron knew nothing of smiling. Erik found it difficult to picture her even with a smirk. "I will send for my allies in the realm. Sven's son Osvald is young—six years old—and perhaps not capable of ruling a nation as great as Badelgard. But Sigmund—hell take him!—is untrustworthy. Osvald has left the capital before Sigmund can kill him; he is in my sister's care in Grinlock Castle."

Erik nodded.

"How many trained soldiers do you have?"

"We have a skilled army of two thousand," Erik said, "and from a levy we can get four times as many untrained."

Greta nodded. "Lord Dagnir Summerleaf is earl of Somerheim. You know this, do you not?"

"Of course."

"He wants an Oster as a ruler as well, and I'd guess he is more than willing to supply soldiers—albeit in secret. He is not altogether happy with Sigmund taking the throne."

"No reasonable man would be happy with Sigmund on the throne," Erik said.

Greta nodded again. She raised her wrinkled hand, which seemed cursed with an ever-present shaking. "You may stay the night here. Tomorrow morning, ride back to Carolyn. You will hear from me soon."

CHAPTER FOUR:
SIGMUND BLACKHELM

The High Throne suited Sigmund Blackhelm well. It demanded wisdom, cunning, and discretion: qualities that Sigmund possessed in bounds. Besides, of all the noble families the Blackhelms were the most honorable and deserving of kingship. The Blackhelms had fought by the High King's side in all the rebellions and squabbles, and it was only fitting and just that one of them should take the throne.

One of the Royal Guard entered. "Your Majesty," he said. "Lady Kenna requests audience with you."

"Let her in," Sigmund said. "*Always* let the Wildsabers in."

The alliance with the Wildsabers benefited both sides. Combined, none of the other five houses could stand against them. It was a wise move.

Lady Kenna entered the throne room, her green gown billowing across the floor and hiding her feet. Mud stained the dress's hem; evidently she had ridden hard. The frown she wore and the redness of anger in her cheeks indicated that the mission to find her son Stenn had not gone well.

"I guess you have not found him," Sigmund said.

"I have not," Lady Kenna said. "The worst news is that the Line of Riverhall is not totally extinguished."

"What do you mean?" Sigmund said. Whether the Line of Riverhall lived on or died off was of no importance to him, though it obviously mattered to Lady Kenna.

"I had forgotten about the Order of Scouts," Kenna answered. "I had forgotten that a few Riverhalls live in what they call the Great Wood. They are possible heirs to the castle and the port. They could challenge your rule."

"No Riverhall has ever challenged a High King," Sigmund replied. "They are soft, lazy, and without honor."

"This one had spirit," Kenna said, "a confidence in his eyes, a challenging air."

"Forget him," Sigmund said. "The Riverhalls are of no consequence."

Kenna's cheeks flashed even redder—a bright red—which Sigmund hadn't thought possible. "They *are* of consequence to me," she growled. "Do not forget our alliance, and how easily it can be broken. Without the support of the Wildsabers, you are *nothing*."

There was a grain of truth to what she said. The Wildsabers possessed a strong army of archers and halberdiers. The Blackhelm army was stronger than theirs, but if a battle ensued between them, the Wildsabers might weaken his forces enough for another family to usurp the throne.

"Leave me," Sigmund said anyway.

Kenna's eyes bulged in anger, and then she stormed off.

That afternoon, a host of insurrectionists faced execution. Most were lowborn; those were flayed alive before the headsman's sword cut off their neck. Sigmund watched from a hidden balcony, reclining in a cushioned chair as he sipped a stein of mead.

Throughout his youth, he had developed a taste for the macabre. At first he felt ashamed at his enjoyment, but no longer. He liked watching executions—the lowborns above all, for those were the best show. The lowborns got what they deserved; they were not descendants of the Seven Wardens and deserved painful deaths.

Up next was Oleg Olegsson, a freeman wheat farmer of Ostergard. Oleg's neighbors claimed that he questioned Sigmund's legitimacy to rule. Each informant received two silver pieces as recompense, and Oleg's land was made a ward of the state.

Sigmund sipped his stein of mead as the torturers flogged Oleg with metal rods. He yawned in boredom and looked over his list. After Oleg came Brandir Albertsson, the scullery rat who added poison to

Sigmund's pottage. The list went on and on.

A wind wafted into the balcony, and Sigmund knew someone had stepped in behind him. Quickly, he drew out his knife and leapt out of his chair. He gulped as he twisted around and thrust the blade outward.

It was Aron Svensson, his chief page, his thick hair full of blond glory.

"Gods." Sigmund touched his shoulder. "You frightened me."

The boy's short-sleeved kirtle revealed the fresh, rosy skin of youth. He had seen less than fourteen winters, and his surname indicated his lowborn status, but Sigmund named him housecarl, and trusted him with his life. Aron was reliable, respectful, and never late. He was a little valkyrie—Sigmund's own little valkyrie.

"Rest your heart, master," Aron said. "You see death in the shadows."

Sigmund smiled whenever Aron called him 'master.' "You are right, my pet. I should rest my heart."

Aron smiled. His teeth were white, bleached with powder. Some might call him a dandy, but Sigmund thought he had the makings of a fine warrior, if he put his mind to it. "Master," said Aron. "An informant has arrived in your court." His soft blue eyes gazed into Sigmund's. "It pains me to tell you the news."

"Tell me the news."

"The informant is one of the Ears of the Realm."

Sigmund smiled with pride. In his few weeks on the throne, he spearheaded the creation of the new spy order.

"He reports of furor in Lady Greta's court."

"Greta Oster, you mean"

"Aye." Aron nodded. "He says she is wroth with you. It seems that not only lowborns are conspiring against you. Some of the Warden-blooded are traitors to Badelgard as well."

Sigmund clutched the arms of his chair with sweaty palms. "They will not defeat me."

Aron touched Sigmund's hand and smiled, revealing the rows of white again. "No one will defeat you."

Sigmund looked away, partially in an attempt to block out Aron's intense smile, and saw Oleg Olegsson's head flying off the executioner's platform. "Are they gathering an army?" he grunted.

"The spy did not say," Aron said. "But pray tell... how many are under your command?"

"With the Wildsabers, and the Silverbacks, and the Trowfells, plus mine, we have ten thousand, at least—"

"The spy says that the Trowfells are wroth with you as well. He says that the Trowfells instigated the rebellion... that Erik Trowfell began it all."

Sigmund wiped some of the clammy sweat off his neck. "We must strike first. The Trowfell conspiracy must be stopped! Send an assassin to kill Erik!"

"You must be kidding, milord," Aron said. "I thought you were a man of honor, not a coward. A man of honor faces his enemies on the field. He doesn't use cloak-and-dagger antics."

"Don't talk down to me, brat!" Sigmund roared. He glared at Aron. How dare the lowly housecarl speak down to him, to a bloody *king*. Sigmund Blackhelm was the king, not Aron. "Do as I said. Erik Trowfell must be assassinated. Give the command."

"Very well, milord," Sir Aron said.

"Now *go*!" Sigmund hissed.

As the sound of Aron's footsteps faded into silence, he reclined once again. Then, seeing his empty glass, he poured some more mead from the bottle and looked out onto the executioner's platform.

In the distance, Brandir Albertsson walked to his death.

CHAPTER FIVE: KAI RIVERHALL

"So... Lord Harald Riverhall is dead," Scoutmaster Frey said after Kai told him the news. "His wife is in exile. The noble house of Riverhall is in tatters. What can be done?"

"Alysse is gone?" said a scout named Arni. "A shame! I always liked that woman. She's the prettiest woman I ever saw."

"She *was* beautiful," Kai reflected. And it was true; many men envied Harald, not only because of his wealth and luxurious abode, but also the fact that he married that stunning woman; that he walked with her on grand promenades across Andarr's Port. Forget the silks and spices of the city—Alysse Riverhall was the port's most valuable resource.

"Yet her beauty was not her greatest gift," Scoutmaster Frey said. "She was a wise and discreet lady. From my visits to the castle, I could tell she did much ruling behind the scenes. And she made wise decisions."

"What about the darklings? Was that a good decision?" Arni snapped.

Kai growled. *Stupid Arni.*

Frey laughed. "The darklings are no one's fault," he said. "You should sooner blame her for the rain than blame her for the darklings."

"Frey speaks truth," Kai said.

"I always speak truth," Frey said.

In time, the sky darkened. The chirping of crickets began. It was summer, but the insides of Woodhome were still cold enough to require multiple blankets. Spring had been winter, and this summer had been spring. So far, the summer weather proved chilly and rainy. Yet despite the cold, the trees sprouted green leaves. The flowers blossomed in the forest, and the bears—may the gods protect Kai—had awoken from their dark dens. The unnatural cold did not seem to disrupt the workings of nature.

Kai shut his eyes. He tried to remember what he had seen in the fern grove above that rocky cliff. Whatever he saw, he forgot. But he knew in his heart that it was terror that erased the memory. He shut his eyes, tried to think, to open up passageways in his mind that he did not wish to see. He reached deep inside, trying to remember that day, going deep into the well of memory.

An image returned to him: something yellow, like crystallized honey. Fur... bearlike fur. He couldn't make sense of the images.

In his mind, he repeated the words he heard. *Sio Soreldi. Cani Orion. Miuru.*"

Late in the evening the sound of the main door slamming open echoed through Woodhome. Kai leapt off his bed, scrambled through his chamber door, and entered into the main room.

Kai's friend Helgun stood there, clothes soaked with rain and covered in mud. He patrolled the Sixteenth Ward today. The fire still burned in the hearth, and its orange light illuminated Helgun, pale and shaking.

"Helgun!" Master Frey had just run out of his own quarters. "You look like you've seen death."

"I have!" Helgun said.

"What did you see?" Frey asked.

"There was a bear-corpse from a few days ago," Helgun said. "It was lying on the forest floor, eaten by flies. I come to it today... and it's gone! So I figure someone's taken it. Then, in the afternoon, I find the bear, and it's standing up with torn-up fur and smelling like hell!"

Several of the scouts gasped.

"It's a darkling bear!" Helgun said.

"The only known darklings are humans," Frey said. "It doesn't seem possible. But go on."

"I started feeling this awful cold," Helgun said, "and finally I couldn't handle it anymore, so I ran off, and it was chasing me. I don't know what happened to it, or if it's still behind me."

"Go sit by the fire," Frey said. "Warm yourself up... then—"

An ursine roar rattled the walls of Woodhome and a huge, fearsome shape appeared in the doorway. Frey swept his sword out of its scabbard as Helgun barreled inside. A few scouts ran out of the doors with their sabers.

Kai hurried back to his room, cast out the door, and grabbed his bow and quiver from the wall. *Aim for the head*, he told himself. Surely if it were true for darkling humans, it was true for darkling bears.

He barreled back into the main room with his bow in hand and fitted an arrow to the string. In life the bear most likely had a black coat; in this state of living death, its hide was loose, gray, and covered with maggot-gnawed sores. His gray gums stretched in liquefied strands as it bared its fangs.

As the sound peaked in volume, it turned to discernible words: *"A herald I am... the Wintry Lord cometh and his sorcery knows no end. Risen from his barrow is he; and he lives again in death!"*

Kai released the bowstring with a twang. The arrow plunged through the darkling-bear's soupy black eye, through the brain, and out the back of its head. The beast roared again, and staggered further into Woodhome. The smell of its rot filled the main hall, a heady miasma. It staggered toward Helgun.

"No!" Kai cried. He dropped his bow, and drew his curved saber. He charged the wounded bear and slashed an inch into the bear's chest, opening up a wound.

The bear turned its black eyes to Kai. It pitched back an arm, claw gleaming in the hearth's light. An arrow launched from Scoutmaster Frey's bow pierced its temple and—at last—wounded on all sides, the bear fell to the floor with a floor-cracking thump.

"Good work," Frey panted. "Now help me drag this thing

outside!"

Outside, they decapitated the darkling-bear: the only way to make sure it would not stir again.

"The threat is averted, for now." There was no relief in Frey's eyes. "Each day, the wood grows more dangerous. The Ulfr weave their dark spells among the trees. In the coming days and weeks we must be cautious, or we will not survive. It is our duty to defend the wood and keep it free of evil. Yet the task grows more difficult every second."

A chill settled over Kai. The forest outside was dark, and who knew what lurked behind the boughs? The wood had turned against the Order of Scouts. The darklings wandered its depths and even the animals were not safe from their power. The Ulfr reshaped the forest according to their dark vision—a Darkling Wood; a sinister reflection of what the Great Wood once was.

That night, as Kai struggled to sleep, a wolf's howl pierced the silence. Whether living or dead, Kai had no doubt it served the Ulfr. The wood was lost; Kai knew that, even if he would never say it to Scoutmaster Frey.

Frey and a few others talked in the main room, plotting their next move against the darklings. Kai wrapped his blanket tighter and sighed. *It's no use. Nothing the Order of Scouts can do will save the forest. The power of the Ulfr grows. We should all leave.*

I should leave by myself, if they will not, he reflected. But to leave the forest was to leave the only home he ever knew. If he left, where would he go? Where would he stay?

He would stay in this forest even as the evil grew; even as the shadow of the Ulfr fell over all of them. He would die just as he lived: a soldier of the Order of Scouts.

CHAPTER SIX:
ALYSSE RIVERHALL

At sunrise, Alysse awoke, struggled into a simple gray hooded cloak—the one she had bought from a simple Oskir tailor and worn to her beloved Brand's execution—and walked out into the cool, damp morning. She knew where she was going; a village about a mile and a half away, Jacquerre, where the knights were quartering.

She walked along the path and left the ducal wood. Soon apple and cherry orchards appeared, as well as a few vineyards. The grass beside the path was wet with dew. In time, the village of Jacquerre—a tight cluster of plaster thatch-roofed houses—appeared on the horizon on a small hill. A tall wooden fence blocked entry.

At the unadorned wooden gate, she unfurled her cloak, revealing herself as the daughter Vis Voraigne. The guards let her through, and she entered.

The village consisted mostly of houses crammed close together. However, after a little investigation, Alysse discovered a large establishment on the top of the hill called Hogshead Tavern. According to the citizens, it was the center of gossip and the site of the night's entertainment.

Alysse entered Hogshead Tavern with her hood covering her. In her humble gray attire and uncharacteristic lack of jewelry, she did not attract immediate attention. This was more a reconnaissance mission than anything else—a sizing-up of her options.

She sat down at the bar and said, "What do you know of Sir Jourmande?"

"What do I know of him?" said the barkeep, a rough-looking woman in a plain gray dress that looked startlingly similar to Alysse's cloak. "He commands a lot of respect among the knights. Don't tell the duke's men I said this… but rumor is, he's much braver than the duke's son, Lourges."

"Really?" Alysse said. "And why do they say these things?"

"Sir Jourmande always leads the charge while Lourges commands from the rear guard. Jourmande has made sacrifices for his soldiers, taken wounds for them; Lourges uses his army as personal shields." The barkeep grinned. "One time—when it was obvious that they respected Jourmande above all—Lourges challenged him to a death-duel. Jourmande is a man of honor and consented. Jourmande won single-handedly, but spared Lourges' life. There was no recovering from that."

Alysse smiled. "And tell me where Jourmande stays around here."

"At night, he's here, drinking with the other knights and some of the soldiers," the barkeep said.

Alysse nodded. "And tell me… what kinds of things does he like?"

"He likes women of the royal class," the barkeep said, then chuckled to herself. "He's always saying he wants to marry one of the king's daughters. Not the likes of you or me. I think he wants to be king of Zarubain. I have a feeling the dauphin won't like that."

Alysse returned home, fit herself into a fine green gown, ate a snack of bread, and walked into the lightless chapel of Umbra. In total darkness she prayed that her mission would go well; that Greatshadowed god would bless his humble servant. Then she walked back to Jacquerre, getting there just before dark. She waited in the tavern for Jourmande. As the evening deepened, more and more people filtered in.

And in time, whispers among the tavern's patrons pointed Alysse to Jourmande himself. The first thing she noticed about Jourmande was the heavy white scars that marred his face. Evidently he had taken many cuts in his career as a knight. He had a swarthy complexion, dark eyes, light brown hair, and a tall, muscular build.

Alysse quietly made her way over to the bar and stood behind Jourmande. "Greetings, Jourmande." Jourmande turned around. She curtsied. "I have heard so much about you. I am honored to make your acquaintance."

Jourmande looked at her in surprise. "And what is your name, lass?"

"Alysse Riverhall, nee Voraigne, and I can make you a king."

"A king?" Jourmande grabbed his pewter wineglass and walked with Alysse, leading her to a shadowy corner table. They sat down. "I've always wanted to be a king. And how would you accomplish this, lass? Are you a witch?"

"My brother Lourges is a coward," Alysse said. "You are three times the man he is. If you come with me to Badelgard—"

"*Badelgard?*" Jourmande said. "An impoverished, desolate nation to the north… snowing constantly. Why should I want to be king of that place?"

Alysse hid her desperation. "There are riches," she said. "There are timber and iron and copper. There are furs. You and I… we could turn Badelgard into a complex civilization. You would be High King… and I, your High Queen."

"And you would be my wife?" Jourmande said.

Alysse lowered her hood. "Tell me you would not marry me."

Jourmande paused a while, looking intently at her face. "You are a beautiful woman," he finally said. "But I do not know if you are a *good* woman. I do not know if you would stab me in the back."

"And with you commanding the respect of the army… why would I stab you in the back? So that the army may turn and slash me to ribbons?" Alysse laughed. "You must be joking, sir."

Jourmande's eyes narrowed. "And how do I know this is not a trap? That you are not working for your brother and trying to somehow snare me into the gallows?"

"I hate my brother," Alysse said. "At best… I find his presence odious. I would never do such a thing."

"And how will we get to Badelgard?" Jourmande said. "Have you thought of that, pretty girl?"

His tone indicated "pretty girl" was an insult. "I *have* thought about it. We will rent a fleet of ships."

"That would cost a king's ransom," Jourmande said.

"The coffers of the House Vis Voraigne run deep," Alysse said. "I have access to the vault. Piles of glittering silver and gold waiting to be taken."

Jourmande's eyebrows furrowed. "Will you betray your family? Cause your noble house to fall into ruin because of your vain ambition?"

Jourmande isn't going to make me feel guilty. "Do you want to be High King, sir, or do you only want to play games? The Line Vis Voraigne can deal with the lost funds; we have gotten through worse."

"But can they get through having no army?"

"They can levy peasants," Alysse said. "And besides... why do you care? Has my brother treated you especially well?"

"I am only thinking of honor... of *your* honor," Jourmande said. "I could care less about what happens to the Vis Voraignes."

"Don't think about my honor," Alysse said. "You have one life to live. Would you like to spend it as the High King, or as my brother's pet hound?"

Jourmande was silent for a long time. Many moments passed, and they only stared into each other's eyes, calculating, estimating. "Gods know, my men will follow me wherever I go," he finally said. "And even peasants know that the soldiers hate your brother. I could say no, Alysse, and wisdom and discretion demand it. Yet I have always wanted to be a king."

"And you will be," Alysse said. "The nation of Badelgard is in turmoil. There is no more perfect time to strike." She paused, looking deep into his eyes. "Yet without my hand in marriage, they will not honor your kingship. You must be a Badelgarder. You must be joined with me... a Riverhall."

"If it comes to that, then I will decide," Jourmande said, "at the time that is right for me. I am not sure I want an ambitious wife who would steal her family fortune—"

His words did hurt Alysse, a little.

"—but perhaps, in time, you will become less unpleasant to me."

"I will send for the ships. If you do not show up, then, *by gods*—"

"I never break my word," Jourmande said. "Furthermore, I swear on my honor."

And Alysse knew that Jourmande took 'honor' seriously.

CHAPTER SEVEN:
ERIK TROWFELL

An army massed in the wilderness, about five miles from High Crag. A thousand swordsmen, five hundred axmen and five hundred archers waited there—all belonging to the Trowfells. As for those who hated the House Trowfell, those who sneered at them in Earls' Court… let them answer to Lord Erik and his rows of soldiers. His enemies would be cut down as they spoke, and their heads thrust on pikes.

Greta Oster had arrived a few hours ago by carriage; her old bones could no longer handle riding. Her red-robed elite guard, plus an army that belonged to Oster descendants across the realm, came with her.

Just now, the forces of Lord Dagnir Summerleaf were arriving. The earl of Somergard was an old man, though not as old as Greta. The gray hair on his head was wisp-thin, yet his beard was full and retained traces of blond against the silver. His garb was poor, but obviously he had made every attempt to appear otherwise. A brass necklace fell from his shoulders, studded with gems—but these were stones of quartz and garnet, unlike Greta's diamond brooch. His leather boots gleamed with polish, yet as he drew closer to Erik, it became evident that holes marred the soles.

"Greetings, Lord Dagnir," Erik said, then bowed deeply in an effort to signify inferior status. It was a habit: Erik's way of ensuring he was always polite.

"Where is Greta?" Dagnir answered as he glanced away.

Even Dagnir Summerleaf—an impoverished, backwater earl—treated Erik Trowfell as beneath him. Then again, Erik got the impression that Dagnir's perception of himself was distinctly different from the perceptions of others. His rudeness was laughable, really—almost pathetic.

"I will be leading the men in battle," Erik snapped. "I expect some proper reverence. Greta seems to have no problem giving it to me, and she is an Oster."

Dagnir's scowl intensified. He struggled for a few moments before grunting, "Aye." Then he walked away.

Dagnir contributed a force of about a thousand soldiers. In all, with the addition of Greta's army, they commanded a force of about six thousand. Greta outfitted every one of her soldiers with steel mail and gleaming red-gold Oster surcoats; Erik provided his elite guard with mail, and the rest with leather jerkins. Dagnir's soldiers, by contrast, wore only canvas shirts. It was pathetic, yet Dagnir obviously fancied himself a mighty lord.

As Erik sat with Greta in her carriage, he confessed, "We will need more soldiers, and better ones."

"Dagnir gave me the impression that he had a much larger army. He says they are well trained, but now I doubt what he says," Greta said. She laid her weak, wrinkled hand on Erik's. Her grey eyes were filled with yearning, and maybe a little lust. "We must gather more."

"We can go to Garn Wildsaber," Erik suggested.

"You are young and still fair of form, so I forgive you ignorance," Greta said, caressing his hand. "The Wildsabers are allied with Sigmund Blackhelm. Their dark alliance is why we Osters did not put one of our own on the throne."

"What of Henrik Silverback?"

"Henrik was on good terms with Sven Oster, so in that regard he has reason for alliance with us. But I have made one too many jests about his piteous holdings. He would never join hands with me. I've burned that bridge, loath as I am to admit it."

"Then where will we gather soldiers?" Erik asked.

"My grandson Brunni has an elite guard. He lives in the east of Ostergard, twenty miles northeast in the shadow of the mountains. His castle is called Mountain Hold. Tell him I sent you, and that we need his aid. He loves his grandmother."

"I will go to Brunni. But try to send for Henrik Silverback anyway," Erik said. "My mother told me that, sometimes, our perceptions of things are wrong. Maybe the jests did not affect him overmuch."

"I would be a fool to ask him," Greta said, "and the rustic Frostfallians do not suffer fools well."

"We need all we can," Erik said. He laid his arm on her shoulder. "Do it for me."

"I will do so if you wish it," Greta said, then stood up and feebly walked away.

Perhaps, Erik reflected, he had asserted himself too much.

Erik rode hard through the afternoon across the barren fields of High Crag and into the depths of the pine forests. Soon the jagged purple mountains appeared. Snow covered the whole extent of the mountains, from peak to the base—so very unusual for summer.

He drew near Mountain Hold. A packed-dirt road wound through the tall green pines and firs. Occasionally, a pig sty, shepherd's field, or small plot of wheat came into view. Yet overall, Erik found the eastern edge of Ostergard quiet: a sparsely-populated, densely-forested place.

Twin flags appeared—bright red and gold—fluttering in the wind on posts: a sign he drew near Brunni Oster's abode. At once Erik began practicing his speech under his breath. He had scarcely gotten through the salutation when someone stepped out of the forest.

He was bald, with a thick black beard, and towering in stature— perhaps seven feet tall. His sword, clipped to his belt and nearly touching the ground, matched his size.

Erik gasped, startled. "Greetings!" He fumbled over his words.

"Are you Erik Trowfell?" the giant said.

"Yes," Erik said, and immediately regretted it. Perhaps this giant was looking for him, and did not mean well. "I mean, no. No, I'm not Erik Trowfell."

The giant laughed deeply. "Where are you going?"

"I am going to Lord Brunni Oster. I am his housecarl. I am… returning from a mission," Erik improvised. He scratched his nose, and his finger returned covered in sweat. "I went to deliver a message, you see."

The giant laughed again, so thunderously that the ground seemed to shake. "If you are a lowborn housecarl, then why do you wear a signet ring? And why does it have the dove of the Trowfells? And why do you wear such fine clothes, stained though they are? And why do you look so gods-damned similar to Carolyn Trowfell?"

Erik couldn't answer any of those questions. Instead, his hand went to the leather hilt of his sword.

In response, the giant yanked his sword—a gargantuan head-cleaver of a weapon—out of its bulky sheath. He roared, "Do not threaten Huge Gunstein!"

Erik jerked his sweaty palm away from the leather hilt. "There is no need for violence!" he whimpered. "You are a highwayman, no? A common bandit? I'll give you money…"

"Huge Gunstein does not want money!" he roared. "Brunni Oster is a friend to the Osters! And King Sigmund is the one who gives Huge Gunstein his hams! King Sigmund does not like the Osters! Don't you see why we are at an impasse?"

"But money…" Erik stumbled over his words. "Money is good!"

The giant's tone turned gravelly and low. "You speak to Huge Gunstein like one touched in the head. Like a child. If you must ask, Huge Gunstein was told to kill Erik. He will enjoy killing Erik very much, because he enjoys killing."

"You know, money can buy lots of hams!"

Gunstein's face flushed red. He bared his rotted yellow teeth, so stark against his blue gums. "You are stupid to anger a man of Adal

Vale!"

Erik knew little of that remote, alpine land. The valemen were known for their quick tempers and berserking ways. Fumbling over his words, Erik said, "I did not mean to anger you!" His sweaty hand was moving slowly back toward the sword hilt. Despite his thudding heart, he prepared his mind for battle, trying to calm himself and focus.

"Make your amends with the gods," cried Gunstein as he pitched back his greatsword, "for you will meet either them or the *demons* soon!"

Gunstein heaved his greatsword toward Erik's head. Twice the length of Erik's longsword, the blade whistled as it hammered down, and in the panic of the moment Erik made his first mistake.

He shielded himself with his longsword in an attempt to parry, but the sheer weight of the giant's sword bent Erik's blade and knocked him to the packed dirt with a force that stole the air from his lungs. He drew a shuddering breath, but no air entered him.

Gunstein cleaved back his greatsword. The death-blow was coming. Wind whistled against the blade. Erik rolled to the right as the blow fell, so narrowly that that the blade sheared a few hairs off his head. Erik yanked his sword backward, and looked up. Seeing Gunstein's feet, he punched the longsword forward in an attempt to hamstring him. The blade glanced off the giant's steel sabatons, and Erik nearly lost his grip on the hilt as the blow diverted.

"Little boy cannot defeat Huge Gunstein," the giant said, and burst into laughter. "Come, now, get up. Gunstein does not normally play fair, but he feels honorable today."

Erik staggered to his feet, fumbling forward as his heart pounded. He cried out as he rushed Gunstein, as he moved in for a hard slash. He did not notice the greatsword swinging down until something struck his right pauldron with shattering force, until the flesh of his right shoulder split open and his bone gave way with a sickening crack.

Even as the wound opened, Erik switched hands, gripping his sword in his left. Breathing ragged, hair moistening with sweat, blood soaking the padding inside his armor and turning it hot, he awkwardly hammered his sword down: pounding, pounding, pounding and only making dents.

At last, Gunstein shoved Erik away with a force that knocked him to the hard ground and made him give up hope. The blood kept pouring, and he got the sensation of swimming as his head grew light and dizzy. Vaguely thinking he was going to die, he watched as Huge Gunstein barreled forward.

Erik staggered back to his feet, and as he did, he ducked. The giant fumbled over him in his heavy steel boots, and stumbled. At last, a hint of luck.

Erik stuck his leg out and the giant tripped. Weakly it occurred to Erik that he held a sword in his left hand. He never fought with his left hand but his right hand would not move. He leapt onto the giant's back, slamming his steel-lined heels into him.

Gunstein deserves no mercy, he thought deliriously. He jabbed his sword into Gunstein's back, and the blade went through. Using all his strength, Erik worked the blade back in forth like a saw, struggling through layers of steel and flesh and stubborn sinew, yet tearing an ever-widening hole through the man's back. Gunstein's shrill screams put a weary smile on Erik's lips despite the heat running through him, the blood pouring out of him. Like a workman he shredded through Gunstein's back, splitting flesh, opening a wide gaping hole.

Eventually, Gunstein stopped screaming.

As quickly as he could in his semiconscious state, Erik removed his armor. He removed his Trowfell surcoat and wrapped it tight around the shoulder wound. It stung as he wrapped it tighter and tighter. All this he did with his left hand. His right arm did not respond to his mind's commands. Gunstein dealt him a wicked wound, but Gunstein was dead. At one point it occurred to Erik that he could not be saved, that not even the Healing House in Trowfell could stop the bleeding. But his delirium quickly swallowed any moments of lucidity.

He struggled onto the horse and goaded it on. The horse trotted back the way he had come. His father was gone and his mother needed him, and he needed his mother. He would abandon Greta and the foolish vengeful mission. He would ride all the way into sweet mother's arms.

Mother.

He died before the first mile.

CHAPTER EIGHT: SIGMUND BLACKHELM

Sigmund sat in his bed and counted the shadows. What secrets hid in those dark places? If someone gained entrance to his bedchamber, his only hope was the thick-steeled Frostfallian dagger under his pillow. Gods knew he could not fare well against an assassin with a spear or one of those long-bladed southern walking swords.

He looked out his window. Outside, through the steel bars, was the city of Oskir. Sigmund had properly subdued the lowborns living in the City of Kings. After days of executions, no one dared whisper challenges to Sigmund's rule.

In the dim light of the doorway, a figure appeared. The satin draped over its body gleamed white in the torchlight. Could this be a fiend, conjured from infernal nightmare and sent to kill Sigmund? He broke into a cold sweat as the figure drew closer.

Soon its face was recognizable as Kenna's. She was in her white bedclothes, hair frazzled and undone. For a reason Sigmund was not conscious of, he shut his eyes and pretended to sleep. Crickets chirped outside. A calm silence filled the room.

She did not leave him while Sigmund was awake. Yet, in the morning, when the skies were gold and red, she was gone.

As the servants dressed him, Sigmund pondered the events of the prior night. He trusted Lady Kenna, yet she had come into his room and waited there as if possessed. It was as if a demon had entered her. King Sigmund could read very little, but perhaps a trip to the royal archives was not out of the question.

Now he wore his purple-dyed, gold-threaded kirtle, and felt comfortable in his fustian, scarlet breeches. The softness of the clothing somehow diffused his unease. Yet in the throne room, despite the fiery hearth, the air held a heavy chill.

A spy arrived in court that morning: a dutiful Ear of the Realm. He brought much news. "The body of Erik Trowfell has been discovered; he is dead. The assassination is complete," the spy said, his face hidden by a shadowy black hood. "An army is marshaling at High Crag, my king. The Osters, Summerleafs, and even Henrik Silverback are gathered under one banner."

"This is horrid news!" Sigmund exclaimed. "We must gather an army to face them. We must strike first. I have enough money to purchase mercenaries. We can lower the Drawbridge… hire a band of horsemen!"

"We don't have time for that!" Kenna's voice called out as she appeared, walking into the throne room from the east wing. She wore a billowing red-and-black gown that reminded Sigmund of a butterfly. Her choice of dress reminded Sigmund of his fashionable first wife—gods rest her soul—before she flung herself off the merlons of Blackhelm Keep.

"Then we must hire every unaligned man we can find," Sigmund said. "Pay them off… and furthermore, Kenna, you must ride to your brother Lord Garn and take all the soldiers he can afford to lose. The Wildsabers and the Blackhelms are one."

Kenna's cheeks flushed red, as if she were angry that Sigmund gave her a command.

Sigmund looked down on her sternly. "I want you to leave, right now."

"What about the girls?" Kenna said.

"I will take care of them." Sigmund looked at the spoiled little imps in his midst. Four little girls of varying ages sat around the throne room, each wearing gold-woven samite dresses and white linen gloves. Their costly attire was bought from an Oskir tailor at Sigmund's expense. The oldest one—ten years old, if memory served—played with a white rabbit. The servants had spent all week cleaning up its droppings.

"Prepare my horse!" Kenna snapped at her servants, who immediately scurried out of the throne room as if chased by a storm.

It was three days before Lord Garn Wildsaber's host arrived, but Sigmund was ready for them. In that span of time, he hired a few hundred mercenaries—some cavalry from the northern highland, a cadre of swordsmen from the river valleys, and a band of pikemen from the mountains. He instructed a few contingents to patrol Ostergard, and a few to protect Blackhelm Keep and Trowheim from insurrection.

Sigmund's army, bearing the proud black-and-gold eagle standards of the Blackhelms, and Lord Garn's army, bearing the yellow-and-white swan standard of the Wildsabers, left for High Crag in early morning.

Lady Kenna rode in the middle of the army resentfully; she wanted to ride in the vanguard with her brother and the king, but in Sigmund's mind it was simply not proper for a woman to lead battles.

Sigmund knew of Kenna's ambition. Not only did he know of it, but he also respected it. Yet he did not want her harmed, and if there were a surprise attack she would be in the front lines. The heads of the highborn families would look down on Sigmund forevermore, saying he let a woman of proud, noble birth die and forced her to ride in the front of an army.

They set up camp in the late afternoon. High Crag lay just a mile away. Here, in the barren moss-land of the southeast highlands, bits of snow and ice lay untried by the summer's warmth. Sigmund sat in his tent, wrapped in furs and sitting on his mattress to ward off the cold.

"Hail!" Sir Aron's voice startled him. He had entered through the tent flap.

Sigmund couldn't help but smile when he saw those long golden locks, those brilliant eyes of blue, those rosy lips. "It is so good to see you, housecarl." He smiled and got up from the mattress.

"I wanted to offer my services, master. What can I do for you?" Aron asked.

"If you wish to earn my favor, then this is what you should do. When the time is right, spy on Lady Kenna and tell me if she is a witch."

"A witch?" Aron's jaw slacked. "All our witch-children are killed according to customary law! Those that survive, we burn at the stake!"

"Kenna has roused my suspicions," Sigmund said. "Therefore, gird yourself with wisdom and discretion. When you enter into her chambers, be cautious."

"Aye," Aron said. "Anything to earn your favor."

At dawn, Sigmund and his army left, moving across the barren moss-land. In time, they arrived. High Crag—a sharp plateau perhaps two-hundred feet high—was abandoned. There were no Oster standards; there were no standards. There was no army at all.

Sigmund gasped. "Has the spy lied? I will have him killed for being so foolish. Ha! I will gut him."

"He is highborn," a low voice corrected. "We cannot gut him."

Sigmund turned his head to identify the know-it-all's voice. Garn Wildsaber rode a few yards away, his light brown hair waving in the breeze. Sigmund realized just how truly little of him he had seen over the journey. Garn was the leader of the Wildsaber forces; a man of many battles—and a warrior who had taken many lives—but he did not know how to properly address a king.

"It does not matter that the spy is highborn. I will have the spy gutted anyway."

"That would be a grave dishonor," Garn said.

Behind him, there was a commotion. Soldiers jeered. Sigmund looked back and saw Lady Kenna forcing her way through the army. "Do not wait here, my king!" she snapped. "For all we know, we could walked into a trap."

Sigmund nodded. The lack of an army here indicated such. "We ride full-circle back to Oskir!"

Halfway back to Oskir, a rider came galloping toward the army. His black hood revealed his identity as a member of the Ears of the Realm.

"The Ears are all liars!" Sigmund shouted.

"I advise you to listen to him, milord," Garn asserted. "They told us what they thought. They did not intentionally lie…"

"We were wrong!" the spy hollered. "So very wrong!"

"*Of course you were!*" Sigmund grasped the hilt of his sword with a shaking hand. "You spies always seem to be wrong."

"It was a trap, and the spy who told you to go there was working for the Osters. You narrowly evaded them. They have since returned to High Crag. You will be well-advised to return and ambush."

"I cannot trust any of you spies!" Sigmund roared.

"I think he is telling the truth, my king," Garn said. "The first person to misspeak was a traitor. Now, a loyal one seeks to correct it."

"Ah! But perhaps he still has some loyalty left over to Sven, and not me."

"Sven is dead," the spy said. "You are High King now. We are sworn by our honor to be loyal to you, Your Majesty."

Sigmund grumbled.

"We turn around and face them," Garn said. "We surprise *them*, though they sought to surprise us."

"Let it be as he says," Sigmund mumbled, and barked orders for the army to turn around.

CHAPTER NINE: KAI RIVERHALL

Kai Riverhall patrolled the Seventh Ward, clammy hands slipping on his bow.

Each step was a battle. The scouts had seen much over the weeks. Darkling bears. Experiences frightening enough that the mind forgot. Howlings in the night. A sense of cold dread all over the forest. Things were not altogether well in the Great Wood. At a more tender age, Kai thought patrolling the woods was boring; the most frightening things were black bears, and those—for the most part—feared human contact. Now the restless dead wandered amongst the trees.

Sio Sorelden. Cani Orion. Miuru.

The day passed slowly. It was silent in the Great Wood, but Kai knew he was not alone. Whatever he had seen—whatever he had forgot—was out there somewhere.

At about noon, a darkling appeared in view. It was a middle-aged woman, her stomach distended not from pregnancy but from eating raw flesh. Kai shuddered, wondering whether the body of a human was in her wretched white stomach. She moved quickly. She was a hopper—one that could dart toward you in the blink of an eye.

Kai drew his curved saber. With hoppers, bows did not work as well; they could dodge arrows with ease. "Come to me, wretched demon!" he shouted.

The darkling-woman turned, looking at him with rabid pink eyes. She barred her teeth and stretched out her sharp black claws. Then she dashed at him, moving as fast as a wolf in full sprint. Kai swung hard with his saber, and the blade bit into her neck. Her head fell, severed, red hair contrasting starkly with the colorless brown-gray of the forest floor.

A morbid curiosity overtook Kai. He had done this before, though not in the presence of other scouts. He cut open the distended stomach and out rolled guts, chewed-up flesh and a shredded head. She had swallowed a large portion of the head whole. Despite the destruction of the head, he could recognize it. It belonged to Arni, the dumbest of all the scouts.

Kai gasped and shuddered. This was not right. No scout had died in a long time. After a moment's hesitation, he sprinted back to Woodhome.

Within the once-cheery pinewood walls lay a scene of carnage. Two scouts in the entrance lay dead, their blood welling up into pools on the floor. Their sabers still lay in their lifeless hands. Their faces were frozen in an expression of abject terror, eyes wide and mouths open. Kai shuddered and questioned whether he wanted to go in.

He needed to be brave. He *would* be brave.

He ran into the main room. The hearth-fire had been put out, perhaps with water, and now the air was too cold for living. The carnage here was even more complete. Guts, intestines, and innards smeared over the log walls. A dozen scouts lay there in pools of blood, their chests torn open as if by claws.

In the distance was the severed head of Scoutmaster Frey. The eyes were poked out, but Kai could tell it was Frey. Kai shrieked. Near the hearth lay the body of his friend Helgun. All the corpses had wide eyes and open mouths, frozen in eternal screams.

A horrible stench hung over all. Kai bent over and vomited all over the once-pristine floors. He stumbled backward, lightheaded and dizzy, and saw, above the hearth, words painted in blood: "*Cani Orion is Lord of the Wood.*"

Kai's heart pounded like a drum. Whimpering, he turned and dashed back into the cold air, into the forest. Now in the First Ward, the absolute center of the Great Wood, he needed to get to the Twelfth so he could run out of the Great Wood, out of Andarr's Port and into the safe towns of the east.

He sprinted past the shadowy pines and thin aspens, wondering if each tree held dark secrets or if strangers hid behind them. Soon his exhaustion caught up with him and he slowed to a jog. His breath grew hoarse as he exerted himself to the fullest.

When he reached the Ninth Ward—heralded by a set of high fern-covered hills—he slowed to a walk. He stopped, keeled over, and panted hard, his throat raw and burning, his entire body drained of energy. He had run for at least three miles at full sprint.

Finally, he stood back up, knowing he had to keep going. Yet a cold had settled into Kai's body, and also into his mind. A familiar feeling of cold dread fell over him, and butterflies played in his stomach. Suddenly he wanted to be out of the silent forest, out of the dark wood where his friends had been slain. He turned around, and there he saw the thing that had frightened him all along. The thing his mind had forgotten in an attempt to protect itself.

In form he was much like a man. His hair was long and greasy, dangling to the shoulders, and sandy blond in color. In shape, he was large and muscular. A film of brown grime covered half his pale skin, as if he had climbed out of muck and tried to wash. He had so much hair he almost resembled a bear. Most chilling of all were his eyes: yellow and so bright it seemed they glowed. His ears were large and pointed. His feet had only two toes, and his hands only four fingers.

This was one of the Ulfr. This was Cani Orion. *Cani Orion* was a name.

"I have been returned to life by the Great Witch and she has given me the gift of man-speech," Cani said in a deep voice. "Praise the Mother! Here is to a new age… an age of eternal winter, and endless cold, and the returning of the dead, and the supremacy of us, the Sorelden. What you in your barbaric tongue call the Ulfr!"

Kai's saber was still in his shaking hand. He ignored the pounding of his heart and charged at the Ulfr wizard. The words repeated through his head: *Sio Soreldi. Cani Orion. Miuru!*

His blade swept toward Cani, but the Ulfr thrust out his hand

and there was a blinding white-blue flash. The saber turned freezing-cold, burning Kai's hand, and he dropped it.

Cani reached toward the sky with both of his four-fingered arms. A nimbus of blackish-blue light grew there. The air around Kai grew dead and sick.

This was magic. This, Kai reflected, was why Badelgarders killed their witch-children. This was why their deaths were necessary.

Not knowing the meaning of what he said, he shouted, *"Sio Soreldi!"*

The nimbus of necromantic power grew in size. Cani's yellow eyes shimmered. His strange four-fingered hands trembled. His doglike teeth grated together. The Ulfr wizard was in a trance.

"Miuru!" Kai finished the phrase.

The nimbus vanished. Cani went flying hard into an aspen trunk, grunted, and fell to the ground unconscious.

Kai hesitated for a baffled second, then took off running. Whatever he had said, whatever he had done, had saved him. The word *"Miuru"* had saved him; if only he could discern its meaning. He had heard the Cani, the Ulfr wizard himself, say it all those weeks ago. Somehow it held power, but Kai couldn't make sense of it.

He sprinted like mad for Andarr's Port.

Finally the sprawl of the longhouses and Riverhall Castle soon appeared through the pine-brush. A darkling army had massed by the shore.

An icy hand grasped Kai's shoulder. He cried out, thinking it was Cani Orion. He whipped his body around and gasped, realizing it was not.

CHAPTER TEN:
ALYSSE RIVERHALL

Alysse grasped the reins of her horse and breathed in the fragrant summer air as she watched the soldiers filter into the great ships. The glorious sight was the product of her hard work. She had ridden her horse to the notoriously seedy Storm Coast to the southwest, and offered a pirate captain seven hundred gold pieces to hire out his fleet. Jacque "Longshanks" Zarobo had agreed readily, and Alysse was not worried about any kind of betrayal; no pirates could overtake her. If anything, the pirates should fear her.

The task of loading men into the cogs was three-quarters done when the sound of pounding hooves reached Alysse's ears. She yanked the reins and wheeled around to face the noise. Lourges and father rode up toward her, eyes burning with wrath.

"My daughter!" cried old Ergould. "What in blazes have you done?"

"You had your chance," Alysse said. "You missed it."

"You fiend!" Lourges said. "Why would they listen to you instead of me?"

"Jourmande listened to me, and they listened to Jourmande. Now these men will come with me to conquer Badelgard," Alysse explained, and laughed coldly. "Sir Jourmande is ten times the man you are."

Lourges drew his sword. "And you are nothing more than Jourmande's pawn."

"Quiet or I'll have my army strike you down," Alysse said. "I asked you to help me nicely. You said my proposition was 'childlike.' So I took my fate into my own hands."

"Do you care nothing about our house?" Ergould said. "Do you care nothing about your father, or the memory of your mother? Do you care about your family?"

"My family never cared about me," Alysse answered.

Lourges kicked the stirrups, lifted up his sword, and began a wild charge. He screamed and bared his teeth, his face red with pure rage.

A group of men-at-arms on horses galloped up to block Lourges' path, forming a defensive wall against Alysse. Before Lourges reached the range of their sharp steel halberds, he yanked his reigns and stopped the charge.

"More proof of your cowardice," Alysse said.

Lourges spat at her.

"Do you have any compassion?" Ergould said. "Or do you only have raw, selfish ambition?"

"You never had compassion on me," Alysse answered him.

Someone rode up behind her on a horse. "The flagship is ready for you," said the voice of Captain Longshanks. "*The Lady Dragon* awaits."

"Goodbye, father," she said, and then glared at Lourges. "And goodbye, brother."

Alysse relished the steady breeze as she stood on the bridge of *The Lady Dragon*. It refreshed her against the thick warmth of summer, made her nerves tingle in ecstasy. Their fleet sailed through the swift current of the River Zaros, propelled forward by a strong westerly wind.

About eight-thousand and fifty men rode in with her on the massive fleet. The fifty knights were all devotees of the same knightly cult, the Order of Marabelle, which revered horses above all creatures. Marabelle, the Zarube name of the horse goddess, was depicted on their shields as a handsome silver mare with bells tied to her ankles.

The knights brought heavy plate armor that no weapon could pierce and cylindrical great helms with frightening appearance. Their weapons were great steel swords that could chop a man in half even in armor. All this, without mentioning the power of their warhorses: thin-furred and totally obedient to the knights unlike Badelgard's hairy, obstinate beasts. When riding on horseback and bearing a lance, the Knights of Marabelle could crush even-heavily armored soldiers. And gods knew the armor of the Badelgarders could not properly be called heavy.

Sir Jourmande stood with her. He, a member of the Order of Marabelle, did not seem especially proud of betraying his liege; yet it was obvious how much he hated Lourges. Alysse could sense it from his half-frown and his dark, brooding air. If—when—he became king, then his negative feelings would not be erased. And their success seemed certain; Badelgard was in crisis from the darklings and the death of Sven Oster. The Badelgarders were weak as they ever had been.

Alysse smiled.

Along the River Zaros were vineyards and fields of golden wheat. Occasionally, a fine noble villa appeared in view—rosy-bricked houses of luxury where the peers of the realm spent easy summer days such as these.

It was mid-afternoon when the towering stone walls of Zarubad appeared in view: the capital city and power-center of the kingdom where His Majesty resided. It was the City of Bridges, built along and around the river's numerous islets.

But what a sight it was: immense townhomes of plaster and tile roofs, ornately-carved arches and colonnades, stone churches ringing the afternoon prayer-bells, gardens of fragrant flowers, and—in the center—the Grand Palace, constructed of fine limestone worn gray by time.

Lourges commanded the ship to pass through the narrow sea-lane where large merchant and military ships were allowed to travel. Forming a single line, the other ships of the fleet followed. The citizens of Zarubad—men in doublets and wide-brimmed hats and women in cote-hardies and chaplets—all according to the latest fashion—paused to gawk at them.

The Lady Dragon drove through the tall waves of the open sea.

They would sail through the night and, with luck, enter the bay of Andarr's Port late the next day. The ships of the pirates were bulky and slow, unlike the small, sleek vessels of the Badelgarders.

"Sir Jourmande," Alysse said as the sun set in twinkling colors over the sea.

"Lady Alysse," answered Sir Jourmande. "What do you want?"

"I only wanted to say your name," she said.

Jourmande was silent.

"I only want to be High Queen." Suddenly Alysse felt a tight, squeezing pain in her lower abdomen. She cried out.

"What is it?" Jourmande asked.

"Nothing," Alysse said. The pain faded. She knew what it was. "Is there a physician on this ship? Any kind of healer?"

"I will send for one," Jourmande said. "He is sleeping right now."

"*He*," Alysse said in distaste as another pain started, slightly longer this time. A tear fell from her eye. She knew what was happening. There was no worse place for it to happen than here.

In the bronze light of the morning, Alysse miscarried. Her child was gone. She would not have a son on the High Throne. She wept, and when she was clean, she retired to her quarters and changed into new clothes. Then she slumped on her bed and wept some more.

Sir Jourmande entered. "I'm sorry for your loss," he said. Whose child was it?"

"It belonged to my dead husband, Harald," Alysse answered through her tears. "And another."

"What do you mean?" Sir Jourmande said.

"My husband Harald was impotent," Alysse said. "I needed a surrogate. Be grateful I trust you enough to tell you that secret."

"And why do you trust me?" Sir Jourmande said.

"I don't know," Alysse said. "Perhaps I shouldn't."

Jourmande looked at her silently. "I am sorry for your loss, milady."

"Thank you. Your words comfort me," Alysse said.

Jourmande frowned. "I suppose you want to be left alone."

"You are right," Alysse answered.

The Sky Cliffs appeared in late afternoon. Upon that impossibly high precipice was the kingdom Alysse had spent all this time planning to conquer. The seas of Badelgard seemed troubled, even this far away. A light mist had formed over the waters, and sometimes, in the cold salt-winds, Alysse thought she heard the whispering of ghosts long-dead.

The air had grown cold since they left Zarubain. Up high on the Sky Cliffs a bit of snow was visible. Snow in summer was unheard-of even in Badelgard. How strangely things had changed. And now, on top of the discomfort, she had to deal with her miscarriage. She wondered if she would ever be able to smile again.

The sound of the salt-winds still troubled Alysse. A sense of dread fell over her as the ship cut through the troubled seas and approached the kingdom she once loved. How badly did she want to go back to the old days with Harald, the summer nights spent in luxury with hearty glasses of wine and crispy roast pork?

And yet, she knew there were opportunities now. She had a chance of becoming High Queen, even if small. Surely by now, the men of Badelgard had defeated most of the darklings. When Brand destroyed the Idol of the Great Mother, they in all likelihood crumpled to ash, never to be seen again.

Sir Jourmande joined her on the quarterdeck. "It's horribly cold here," he said. "And there's something in the air... something that doesn't feel right about it."

"Everything is right about it, Sir Jourmande," Alysse said. "The land is ours for the taking."

Soon they passed Death Falls where the southwestward-leading White River crashed into a series of sharp rocks. Crossing Death Falls was impossible; though some fools had tried, all who attempted it had died.

As they sailed on, Alysse admired the sheer rock cliffs, the misty fjords and the stony shores of her adopted homeland. The land of Zarubain was warm and idyllic—yet it was soft and without honor.

The first sight of low land was the pine-aspen forest that extended southwestward from Andarr's Port. In that vast, untamed realm, the Order of Scouts kept themselves busy on patrol. The aspens had grown a new set of green leaves, rustling in the wind, but in time they would don their yellow autumnal wardrobe.

They rounded the sandy shore of the pine-aspen forest.

The pirate captain who owned the ships, Longshanks, walked up to Alysse. "The river's too shallow," he grunted. "Not nearly as deep as the Zaros. We'll have to drop anchor and send you off into the port on smaller boats." He turned his ruddy, whiskery face toward Alysse. "I want the payment now."

"You will get the payment when we are all landed," Alysse said firmly.

Captain Longshanks stepped closer, scowling. His hand touched the hilt of his cutlass. "I want my payment *now*," he growled. "Give it up or I will slit your pretty white throat."

Sir Jourmande, walking up behind him, drew his sword and made his presence clear. "Careful, captain," he said. "This blade has felled stronger men than you."

Longshanks' eyes bulged in rage. He took a cautious step back. "Payment now, or I will kill you both."

"Payment when we *land!*" Alysse growled.

There were perhaps twenty soldiers that belonged to her on this ship, and forty pirates. The pirates, however, were not heavily armored. The best of them wore hauberks and steel caps, and most of them only had leather jerkins.

"Kill him," Alysse said after her careful estimation. The seven hundred gold pieces could come into use. Pirates were the lowest of villains and totally deserving of whatever they received.

"What?" Sir Jourmande said and almost failed to see Longshanks charging at him with his drawn cutlass.

Almost. Jourmande blocked with his shield, and with a flick of his sword, disarmed him. "Surrender," Jourmande said. "You get your payment at the shore."

Longshanks knelt before him. Secretly—but not secretly enough—he reached for a steel dagger in his boot. Jourmande's sword came hammering down and rent his skull in two. Bits of brain and blood flew into the air.

"Should have worn a helmet," Alysse said.

The other pirates, seeing this, charged Alysse's soldiers who were for the most part, surprised and unprepared. Sir Jourmande raced down the creaky wooden stairs to the main deck, his full plate armor flashing in the red sunlight.

A pirate thrust a spear at Sir Jourmande as soon as he reached the main deck, but the steel head glanced off his left pauldron. Sir Jourmande made a hard cross-slash and beheaded him in one blow as another pirate came to take his place. Soon all Alysse's soldiers had either died or flung themselves into the water. Around twenty pirates remained alive. They all charged Sir Jourmande.

Sir Jourmande blocked blows with his shield and counterstruck with his sword. He flung men into the water, cut men in half, and beheaded several more before finally they cornered him and began driving him back. A few of the pirates had sharp, armor-piercing spears, and Sir Jourmande had no chance of escape; if he leapt overboard, then the armor would drag him into the briny depths.

"Stop!" Alysse cried.

A dozen pirates remained. Sir Jourmande fought as vigorously as ever, but the blows struck his armor with increasing frequency. The pirates were experienced fighters, even if they did not have as much experience as the knight.

Eleven. Ten—killed with two quick cuts. Jourmande bashed another with a shield and sent him overboard—nine. Eight—a beheading. Seven—a chest-opening slash.

A spear bit into Jourmande's armor and sank into his flesh. He cried out, retaliating with a shield-blow and sending the spearman overboard. Six pirates now remained.

Sir Jourmande, seeing the enemy's numbers dwindling, fought with more fury than before. He was like an animal, roaring as he pounded them with multiple cuts and slashes.

Five—a heart-shredding stab. Four—another beheading.

The remaining three, seeing Jourmande's rage, ran to the edge of the deck and threw themselves overboard.

"Jourmande, love!" Alysse said. "You are a lion. We have overtaken *The Lady Dragon* through the strength and vigor of one great man."

The other ships had caught wind of the treachery. Battles began on the other eleven ships. The pirates were outnumbered, out-armored and out-armed. As Alysse waited for the—in her mind—inevitable victory, she looked at Sir Jourmande's spear-wound. A bit of blood dribbled down his plate armor.

"Will it fester?" Alysse said. "We cannot have our future High King die. Gods! Let it not be so."

"I have dealt with far worse wounds, milady," Jourmande grunted. "My body is strong."

"Indeed, it is."

Alysse's belief turned out to be correct. The soldiers in the other eleven ships overtook the pirates and cut them down. Alysse and Jourmande got in a small boat and told the others to do the same and follow them.

They paddled across the sea-waves and, after a quarter hour's rowing, reached the calmer waters of the bay. Many more small ships followed them, filled to the brim with knights and soldiers.

Soon the abandoned buildings of Andarr's Port appeared in sight. A light rain began, and a chill infused Alysse's heart as she saw that an army of darklings waited for them.

CHAPTER ELEVEN
SIGMUND BLACKHELM

No trees grew on the flat plain surrounding High Crag. Only moss and lichen—brown and yellow—clung to the sheet of dark black rock. Sigmund's servants had just finished setting up his tent on a small hillock near the center of the area: a perfect observation post. Archers stood just below the tent, and behind them stood Sigmund's personal bodyguard, ready to shield him from the enemy's arrows.

The enemy army appeared, at first as a shadowy form on the horizon and then taking shape. They were vast in number. Here the two armies—the traitors, and the true High King—would fight near High Crag, that ancient field of war where the Wardens did battle long ago.

The size of the opposing army nearly matched Sigmund's own. But none could match, in craft, the Wildsaber halberdiers at the left and right flanks of the army; nor the Blackhelm axmen at the center that fought like bears on the battlefield. Alongside either army, hundreds of mercenaries waited for Sigmund's orders, their steel mail glittering in the cloudy light.

Sigmund himself sat in a chair just outside the tent, with Lady Kenna by his side.

At last, the army became visible. A standard towered high in the center—the blue-gold maple leaf of the Summerleafs, who had an army of about a thousand. Some of them wore suits of mail, and others wore leather.

The White Wolf standard flapped to the left of the Summerleafs. There, the army of Henrik Silverback rode: horsemen in dark jerkins and bearing swords. They wore their hair unshorn, and their beards long and untrimmed.

To the right of the Summerleafs marched the Osters. Their flag—a gold rooster on a red field—rode higher than the others. The Oster swordsmen at the vanguard bore shields painted richly in red and gold, so as to clearly show their allegiance. Greta Oster had deep pockets, or so Sigmund had heard, and could richly outfit the army.

The figure of Henrik Silverback rode out of the front lines on a white charger, sword girt by his side and black leather jerkin covering his chest. The meager armor confirmed Henrik's reputation among the nobles as the 'Poor Man of Badelgard.' He was riding out of the army, into enemy lines.

From Sigmund's own army, Garn Wildsaber rode out to meet him.

Garn and Henrik Silverback talked for a while. Then Garn wheeled his horse around and rode toward Sigmund and Kenna, pushing his way through rows of soldiers as he made his way up the hillock.

Slowly his large, muscular form, his long blond hair and blue eyes became clearly visible, and he was within speaking distance of Sigmund. "Milord!" Garn shouted. "Henrik has a request. He wishes to make a deal."

Sigmund scoffed. A backstabbing trick, if he'd ever heard one. No; there could be no deal with Lord Henrik. Sigmund was determined to crush them all, and eliminate every one of them; then, and only then, would the people of Badelgard respect him. "I do not make deals or treaties," Sigmund said.

"Listen to him before you decide anything, king," Kenna snapped.

Garn frowned. "Their request is reasonable. Lord Henrik, Lord Dagnir and Lady Greta will honor your kingship without a fight if you pay them each five-hundred pieces of gold."

"A good deal," Kenna said. "You'd be wise to take it, and a fool not to. Your coffers as High King run deep, and comparatively, fifteen hundred pieces of gold is a pittance."

"If I pay them and do not crush them, they will betray me when they get the chance," Sigmund repeated. "Besides, it is not the way of the proud Blackhelm warriors. We do give in to silver tongues; we fight."

"Your pride will be the end of you," Kenna predicted.

Sigmund looked into Kenna's sullen brown eyes and glared. He growled his response. "To have pride is to have honor; and honor, I assure you, will not be the end of me." He turned back to Garn. "Go! Tell the soldiers to charge. Crush them!"

Not long after Sigmund gave his command, Sigmund's army—and subsequently, the enemy—ran toward each other. The roars of the soldiers soon grew deafening. They crashed into each other like ocean waves, and the Blackhelm axmen went into frenzies, slashing wildly with their weapons. The Wildsaber halberdiers kept their enemies at a distance as they slashed and stabbed with their long pole-arms. The sounds of shouting and clanging metal filled the air and put the din of the camp firmly in the background.

The battle sat at a standstill for the first hour, with neither side gaining the upper hand. The strong warriors of either side picked off the weak. It struck Sigmund that the Oster army fought with the most skill, the Silverback army with the most honor, and the Summerleaf army with the least of both. Sigmund watched, his muscles tense despite knowing that his side was stronger, confident that he would win.

As the battle progressed, Sigmund found himself looking away at points. The rebel army made inroads into the Blackhelm ranks. The axmen of the Blackhelms fought like savage bears, but they lacked defensive skill. Sigmund watched as his entire body grew slick with sweat. Occasionally he glanced down at his horse, making sure it waited there at the base of the hillock in case he needed to flee.

The winds of fortune changed suddenly. Dagnir Summerleaf's army retreated, and Sigmund's army charged with renewed vigor. In the space of half an hour, the enemy lost thousands of soldiers, and Sigmund's army lost hundreds. Both sides, by now tired from battle, paid less attention to defense and more to ending the struggle. The Wildsaber halberdiers cut into the fleeing Summerleafs while the Oster swordsmen cut into the Blackhelm axmen with equal ferocity.

Sigmund laid a hand on his heart. Several times he stood up, thinking he would ride away on his horse, but always sat back down.

Yet soon the power of sheer numbers ended in Sigmund's favor. The rebel army, now scarcely a hundred strong, began to retreat. Victory was near. Yet in losing, they had cut Sigmund's army to the bone.

A messenger ran up the hillock and proclaimed that Lord Garn fell in battle. Sigmund cried out, "Let it not be so!" and clutched his heart. Yet Lady Kenna—standing behind him—despite being her sister, was calm and said nothing.

It occurred to Sigmund as he surveyed the blood-drenched plain that Henrik was dead, dealt a fatal wound in the heart, his heavy armor drenched in blood and gristle as he lay lifelessly on the battlefield. Greta Oster was gone, and Lord Dagnir Summerleaf, too. The last of the rebel soldiers battled to the death.

"You were wrong," Sigmund said loud enough for Kenna to hear. "My pride is not the end of me. I was right not to surrender to the lords' demands."

"But at what cost?" Kenna snapped.

She spoke truly. Perhaps a thousand of Sigmund's men remained alive. It would be difficult to keep the kingdom in line with that few soldiers; and yet, no resistance remained.

Sigmund smiled as the red-gold Oster flag fell from the standard bearer's hands. It flapped in the wind as it fell, a symbol of their defeat.

The Oster dynasty was no more. The Blackhelm dynasty was now.

Blood transformed the mossy land to a crimson marsh. Bodies

layered the rock like a thick carpet. Severed arms, legs, and heads lay strewn about everywhere. Vultures circled overhead in anticipation for their feast. It was a scene of blood and death. But above all, it was a scene of victory. A victory won at a hard price, but now, Sigmund knew his reign was secure. In time he would capture Dagnir and Greta, and thrust their heads upon the Oskir gateposts.

Sigmund wandered this new landscape. As he surveyed it, a hand touched his shoulder.

Kenna stood there. "All is not well."

"Not well for you and your house, you mean," Sigmund said. "Not well for the Wildsaber halberdiers that were massacred. Only your archers remain."

"Not well for all of us," Kenna answered him. "A messenger has just arrived, riding hard from the west. Lady Alysse Riverhall has returned with an army of soldiers. She intends to usurp the throne."

A chill ran up Sigmund's spine. His heartbeat quickened.

"How dare she?" he screamed. "That she wolf! That...!" He balled his fists. He screamed, and he screamed again.

INTERLUDE I:
KENNA WILDSABER

Kenna cast open the doors of the Golden House. Sigmund sat on the throne, and he had not died as she wished. But in this land of woman-hatred, there would be no position of High Queen for her, even if he did die. Yet there was something that Kenna *could* do, and it all could be done with her craft—the craft that remained illegal.

She went to her quarters. As she walked by the soldiers, she could feel the tension in the air. She set her grimoires on the table. She had read the wizarding books of the south—they all said to avoid the Black Mist that Kenna saw in her mind's eye, saying it was 'Forbidden.' Yet *these* books, purchased from a renegade wizard, told her she could tap that source of limitless power. They told her she could use that endless wellspring to make her magic even more powerful. The warnings of the pious and the prudish meant nothing to Kenna.

"I will call for you, Ulfr witch," Kenna mumbled to herself. "I will call for you, and you will answer."

If I need to join the Ulfr to become High Queen, then so be it, she thought. The voices from beyond the Black Mist told her as much.

She opened *The Black Art* and flipped to the proper page. Here was an explanation of the method of spirit-calling... communicating at a distance of up to a hundred miles through the Black Mist. It took a sacrifice consecrated to Lord Baaoul, demon-prince of sloth. She needed something living to perform the ritual.

The children? Not the children, she decided after a few moments' thought. Those girls had a pet rabbit which they loved dearly. Rabbits had no value.

She fetched the rabbit. Then she hammered her black athame through the squealing rabbit. There was a loud screech and the air grew cold. Gooseflesh slowly formed on Kenna's skin. She shut her eyes and felt a figure rising out of the Black Mist like a dark cloud. She spoke, "Let me speak with the Ulfr witch."

Kenna's legs gave out and she fell to the floor. It seemed to her that she was in an infinite white expanse. A woman appeared in her mind's eye, her face hidden by a hood. "What do you wish of me?" she said, her voice a low growl.

"Make me High Queen of Badelgard," Kenna said, "and I will join with the Ulfr."

A laugh issued from behind the hood: a deriding laugh that made Kenna's face flush in anger.

"You say I should make you High Queen," the witch said, "and you offer what in return? Your good wishes? A pat on the head? What a deal you are offering, Kenna Wildsaber!"

"Do not speak to me so," Kenna hissed. "I am highborn."

"I am higher born than you," said the witch. "I possess far more magical talent."

"Lies!"

"Compared to your pathetic illusion-making, I am a goddess nearly on the level of the Great Mother," the witch said with a laugh. "Yet there is one thing even you can do to curry favor with me."

"Enough favor to make me High Queen?"

"Yes," the witch said. "It is a challenge of sorts. Only a wise, shrewd woman could accomplish the deed."

"I'm listening," Kenna sneered.

"You must kill Sigmund Blackhelm without using any magic; you must make it appear natural, and no one must suspect you," the witch said. "Prove your resourcefulness to me, and I will deem you worthy of High Queen."

"Very well," Kenna said. The woman and the white landscape disappeared; the cloud-figure fell back into the Black Mist like a sunken ship into sea, and Kenna was back in the Golden House, lying on the floor. She drew a cold gasp, and stumbled to her feet. She turned around.

Standing in the doorway was a boy—the housecarl, Aron. He had seen everything.

CHAPTER TWELVE
KAI RIVERHALL

The ice-cold hand touching Kai was the last thing he remembered before he awoke inside the Ulfr home.

The makeshift hut was built of sticks, leaves, and clay. Despite the primitiveness of the dwelling, it did a surprisingly good job of warding off the cold. Sitting on a log across from Kai was a man. His ears were at slight points, obviously nonhuman, yet distinctly un-elven. His eyes were blue unlike Cani's yellow. And yet, judging by his two toes and his four fingers, he was at least part Ulfr. The stench of rot hung around him.

Kai struggled toward the small exit but quickly realized his feet and hands had been bound with rope. "What do you want from me?" Kai screamed as his heart pounded in his throat. After a second's thought, he cried, "*Miuru!*"

"Be calm, friend," the man said in a thin, airy voice. "My mother was Ulfr, and my father was one of you. But it is not my Ulfr blood protects me from the wizards' power-words of death. You have used the Magic Word today; you cannot use it again until the next sunrise."

"Let me out!" Kai shouted.

"Calm yourself," the man said. "I have a human name. I am Leif Helgursson. Does that calm you at all?"

"Not at all," Kai answered.

"Don't fear. You are just a boy, and I do not harm children," Leif said. "Others of my kind might sacrifice children, but I do not. I am not wholly evil; I am not wholly Ulfr."

"Your name is Helgursson," Kai said. "And are you—?"

"I was raised from the dead with the witch's Greatspell. I am reanimated, living yet not entirely living," Leif said. "My father is none other than Helgur, one of the three patriarchs of the human Badelgarders. In all likelihood, you have a little of my father's seed in you. Perhaps we are related."

"What do you want from me, Leif Helgursson?"

"Cani Orion is aptly named; he is vicious and heartless," Leif said. "*Cani* is 'bear' in the Sorelden tongue."

"Sorelden?"

"Aye. What you call the Ulfr, called themselves the Sorelden; and their land, Sorelda," answered Leif.

"And what do you want from me? I must know."

"I wish to defeat Cani Orion. You see," Leif said, and his Ulfr features darkened, "the Great Witch's spell was cast over all the land. Every Ulfr with enough of his spirit remaining was brought back to undeath. Cani Orion wants to kill me. I am a half-breed—an 'abomination'—in his eyes."

"And how could I possibly kill an Ulfr wizard?"

Leif smiled, making his protrusive canines more obvious. "What is your name?"

"Kai Riverhall."

"In truth, your name should be Kai Dragon's-Son. In you is the blood of dragons," Leif said. "You alone can defeat Cani Orion and heal this wood. You alone can save my life."

"Dragon's-Son?" Kai said incredulously. "How could a human have dragon-blood in him?"

"You are correct in saying that dragons cannot breed with humans. Yet dragons *can* bestow a blessing. Before he left, the Green Dragon blessed your ancestor, Folkvar Hjartasson." Leif flashed that long-toothed smile once more. "The reason why you survived Cani's attack is because of that blessing. The Green Dragon's blessing was passed down to you through a direct line of descent— it is carried through the mother.

"Cani Orion is the greatest wizard I know of. His words of power can kill brown bears. But they cannot kill dragons, or Dragon's-Sons."

"How do you know this?" Kai said, still clutching to a trace of unbelief. It all seemed so unlikely.

"I knew Folkvar Hjartasson. I knew his wife, Astrid. And I am sensitive in magic—I can sense that you have some of his blood in him. And when I heard—as all the undead creatures of the wood did—that you survived Cani's attack, then I knew for certain. You are the blood of the Green Dragon."

Kai looked down at the cold earth in amazement. "Me? Dragon's-Son?"

"If you harness your powers enough, you can be like the dragon," Leif said. "You can breathe the flame of the dragon, and learn to leap to impossible heights, as if you are flying with the wings of the dragon."

"You are part Ulfr," Kai said, "so why don't you want me to fail?"

"Part-Ulfr I am, but part-human as well," Leif said, "and my loyalty lies to my better half."

"How do I breathe the flame of the dragon?"

"You must learn to harness the dragon within, and that is the hardest task of all. And to learn the way of Fire and Salt, you must be thrust into that world. With my assistance, you must go to the Ice Shelf. You must retrieve an Ulfr rune-stone from the Seat of the Great Mother; there, you will learn their words of power and turn their dark witchery against them." Leif's eyes grew wide. "Trolls are on the Shelf. The Order of the Green Dragon has journeyed there, but I think their years of devotion and toil do not translate well into troll-slaying."

"The Trowfells of old were known as troll-slayers," Kai muttered as he stared into Leif's strange eyes.

"I do not know of any Trowfells," Leif said. "The mightiest troll-slayer was your descendant, Folkvar Hjartasson."

"The Trowfells are one of the houses descended from the Seven Wardens. But I suppose the Wardens came about long after you died."

"And likely, long after the trolls were buried in a thousand pounds of ice," Leif said. "The Trowfells are no more troll-slayers than the lowborns." He smiled and flashed his unsettlingly long Ulfr teeth again. "They are nothing."

"Saying that would get you killed in their territory," Kai replied.

"Forget the highborns and the Wardens," Leif said. "We are all equal in the view of Nature. Bloodline means nothing."

"I suppose that is what the Ulfr think."

"It is simply the truth."

The Great Witch, Kai learned, had cast a powerful spell over the entirety of Badelgard, so that any Ulfr with a part of his body remaining was raised from the dead. But centuries' rot had ensured that few Ulfr bodies remained remotely intact.

"And yet," Leif said as they set out with their packs toward the Ice Shelf, "if the Great Witch's power as a necromancer grows, even the Ulfr without any flesh or bones left will return... and it will be as it was before humans, albeit in a much bleaker, more deathly existence."

"Bleaker than prior Ulfr society?" Kai said. "I can't imagine."

At Andarr's Port, Kai and Leif crossed the river so as to get on its northern side. Then Kai bade goodbye to the empty, deteriorating houses and shops.

As they passed by the miniscule villages, the air grew colder. An hour into their journey, it began to snow.

"This is bloody *summer!*" Kai screamed. "I've never seen a summer where it snowed... unless you've somehow spirited me through time. But the leaves are bloody *green*, so I know that isn't true!"

Leif smiled. "Harness your rage; for that is the way of Fire and Salt. Anger is the dragon's essence. It is his ever-present emotion—all consuming."

Kai took his advice. "It's summer! It's bloody *summer!*" he repeated over and over at the top of his voice. But he neither breathed fire nor sprouted wings and flew.

"It must be true rage," Leif said, sensing Kai's disappointment. "It cannot be manufactured. It must consume you like a fire."

"Shut up!" Kai screamed out of genuine irritation, and felt a weight swell up inside him.

Leif smiled again, wider than the last time. "Do not consume *me*, Dragon's Son."

They began a sharp ascent up the side of the steep river valley. If it was snowing in warm, seaside Andarr's Port, Kai dreaded the thought of what the uplands would look like.

When they finally reached it after several hours' strenuous climb, they saw that the snow had piled up significantly more—up to Kai's heel. "I have a feeling this is the continuation of an eternal winter," he said.

"The crops will die of this frost, I am sure," Leif said. "The people will starve. And that is why I must train you. That is why the Dragon's-Son must bring an end to it."

Kai did not want this burden—not at all—but no one picks the path their life takes. Lady Vana chose him to be the Dragon's-Son. So, too, had the Dragon himself picked him. "I wish it were not so," he said aloud.

The next day, the white ice of the Shelf appeared in the horizon. Above it was a black, swirling cloud. A million glittering snowflakes fell from it onto the Shelf, looking gray in the cloud's shadow.

Kai's gut grew light, airy. The cold finally got to him. He began to shake. He wanted to run away, but something had awoken inside him—something born of fire, light, and salt. A hatred for the Shelf and the dark cloud consumed him. He wanted to exterminate every living thing that walked the Shelf. He wanted—

"Kai," Leif said, "You are shaking. Are you ready for this?"

"Yes," Kai said. "By Skruga, I will kill every living thing under that cloud!"

Snow swirled around them as they climbed onto the Ice Shelf's slippery, frozen surface. Snow got in Kai's face, onto his back, into his lungs.

He gazed into the bleak, uniform landscape. "There is something out there," Kai said. "I can hear it…" It was a low hum.

"It is not a troll you hear," Leif said. "It is power. It is the energy of the Seat of the Great Mother. The trolls are bringing back her Seat—pulling it out of the ice."

Kai shivered and bent over to vomit. Nothing came out of his mouth, but the retching did take the sharp edge off the fear. "Gods," he said. "Vana… Skruga…"

"Do not say those names here," Leif said. "It will make the trolls come for you. It will make them angry with you."

Kai shook some snow off his cloak. "Okay," he said.

Leif brushed his back. "Now get out your weapon, Kai. There is no worse fate than fighting a troll unarmed."

Kai drew his curved saber, and kissed the blade. It had turned cold, as cold as the ice he trod on.

A shape was coming out of the darkness. It was huge, twice the height of Kai—a dark shadowy silhouette against the gray, swirling snow. Two yellow lights like lanterns shone from it: eyes. Its steps were lumbering, unwieldy.

"Here you are," Leif said. "Will you be Kai Troll-Killer, or will you die, frozen forever in this unholy place?"

CHAPTER THIRTEEN: ALYSSE RIVERHALL

The army of darklings fell quickly to Alysse's army, as she had predicted. The few wounded men were killed, under the reluctant but firm instruction of Jourmande. Then they began marching up the path that led east, following the river. They set up camp a mile outside Andarr's Port, in the thick, aspen-filled area on the north side of the river.

Alysse sat down by Jourmande in the light of a campfire. "We go to Wildsaber Keep," she said. "Tomorrow, we will lay siege to it. We will claim it for the House Vis Voraigne... we will make the people serve us."

"Sometimes, in war, you must act forcefully," Jourmande said. "Do not begrudge me, milady, if there are not many survivors."

"Do you intend to hack and burn your way through Badelgard?" Alysse said.

"I am general," Jourmande asserted. "I make the choices in war."

"First, we must purchase mercenaries," Alysse said. "We have enough gold to double the size of our army."

"You are right," Jourmande said, sounding insulted that she had made a good suggestion. "Where will we find them in this hells-blasted place?"

Alysse suddenly had the urge to be cautious. "I don't know if there are any," she lied. If something went wrong, perhaps she would need that coin.

"Tomorrow, we lay siege to Wildspear—"

"Wildsaber Keep," Alysse corrected, and smiled at the shame it would bring to Lady Kenna.

The army reached the Waterwood the next day. The sycamores had donned their summer wardrobe, their leaves as green as grass. Geese and ducks swam through the lily-covered waters, and shrews poked through the thick, leafy growth of the few bits of dry ground. Some fishermen were out in canoes. As they paddled away in fright, Jourmande ordered the archers to pick them off.

Alysse urged him to stop; urged him to have mercy on these poor, innocent men and women. But he gave the order regardless, not listening to her, not respecting her as the Daughter Vis Voraigne, his liege.

Any travelers they met, too—and there were several heading in either direction along the path—Jourmande's archer picked off as they ran. As it always was in war, a few managed to escape their arrows. Alysse thanked Umbra for their spared lives; and she prayed silently that the Greatshadowed One would protect many more.

Finally, the army reached Wildsaber Keep: a wooden fortress, built on an artificial hill that rose above the water. What soldiers could fit massed around the palisade walls, bearing the standards of the House Vis Voraigne. A white-faced, sheepish-looking man with long brown hair stepped onto the battlements. On his head, he wore an undecorated iron spangenhelm and over his shoulders he wore a hauberk that stretched to his knees. In his hand he held a spear.

They're obviously unprepared, Alysse thought.

"You are obviously not from Badelgard," said the sheepish man, doubtlessly some minor captain filling in for the actual general. "Though I do recognize Lady Alysse. And to her, I say, you should not be here. You are in exile."

"You are in no position to reprimand me, churl," Alysse shouted. "We have with us eight thousand men."

"Open the gates and we will have mercy on you!" hollered Sir Jourmande.

"What are your terms?" the man called out again.

Sir Jourmande trotted a little closer on his huge charger. "Open your gates, or there will be no mercy," he said. "You have until the count of ten to give the order. Ten… nine…"

The man barked the orders from the battlements. A few moments later, the gates began cranking open.

"Charge!" screamed Sir Jourmande.

He does not fight with honor, Alysse thought.

The pounding of hooves filled the air like a roll of thunder. The gates were open and could not be closed. Alysse smiled at the victory, and hoped to Umbra that Kenna Wildsaber was in there. She did not want her to die by the blows of the knights, however; she wanted to deliver the king's justice—a hanging or beheading, as traditional law demanded. Her justice, unlike Kenna's, would be done with honor.

She waited outside the gates on her horse, not wanting to see the battle. She did not enjoy seeing the deaths of soldiers, as some did. The spilling of blood, the screams of dying men, only served to make Alysse uneasy.

Eventually the hooves ceased their pounding, the screamings stopped, and the cloud of dust the knights drew up had settled. Alysse rode slowly into Wildsaber Keep, pushing through the ranks of the army. In the wake of the knights' charge was a scene whose bloodiness Alysse neither expected nor condoned.

Men, women, and children alike had been slaughtered, lying about in bloody pools. Limbs scattered across the ground. By the looks of it, at least a thousand were dead. Several fires had started in the thatch roofs of the houses.

Incredulous, she kicked her stirrups and forced her way up to Jourmande, who was standing before the walls of the inner keep. "What is this?" she shrieked. "No Badelgarder will respect me as High Qu—"

"Silence, woman," he sneered. "If I had shown any mercy, *then* they would not have respect for me. Jourmande diu Jalerce is their king and they will learn as much."

"And I am their queen!" Alysse shouted. "So you listen to me, *Jourmande,* when I say that you will *not* massacre innocents."

Jourmande's eyes narrowed to slits. "You are not a queen yet, Alysse Vis Voraigne, and I am not sure I want you for a wife."

Alysse laughed in disbelief. "You mean I pay for pirates to ferry your gods-damned army up here, to *my own* home, and this is what you do?"

"You did not pay them. Remember?" Jourmande replied.

"Why, you ungrateful wretch!" Alysse cried. She felt her face flush. "You *gods-damned*—

"Bind her and take her away," Jourmande ordered nonchalantly.

Alysse, stricken with awe, stayed silent as a pair of knights bound her hands with rope and forced her off the saddle. Tears formed in her eyes, but her expression stayed the same. She was led off to the tents, realizing that Jourmande was a lion untamed and she was a poor tamer. She walked with her captors as they led her to the main tent.

Late that night, they finally cut her binds. Only then did she make noise—a loud, shuddering gasp. "I am Alysse Vis Voraigne."

"And he is Jourmande the Lion," responded the youngest and poorest of the Knights of Marabelle, Sir Gorbande. Around his set of thick brown hair, he wore a cheap chainmail coif and in his hand he grasped a spear of poor make; doubtlessly those items were all he had.

"I am a duke's daughter," Alysse said firmly.

"Not a good one, though," sneered Gorbande. "If my daughter did what you did, I would disown her."

Only after those words did Alysse let the tears fall. She wept into her sleeves.

Early the next morning, Alysse put her feelings aside and walked back into the ranks of the army. Someone had appeared at the window of the inner stone keep. He was a young man, perhaps twenty years old, and wore a surcoat with the yellow-white swan flag of the Wildsabers.

"My father Garn is not home!" he hollered. "He is fighting traitors to the realm!"

"Come out of the keep, now!" shouted Journande. "Leave your weaponry inside. If you pledge your loyalty to King Journande diu Jalerce, then we will spare your lives. If you refuse, we will burn you at the stake."

"Burning at the stake is a barbaric southern practice!" shouted the young man. "I can tell by your strange horses and your strange armor that you are from there... but I am highborn. Death must be delivered painlessly."

"There are no painless deaths to those who fight against me— highborn, lowborn, or born in heaven!"

A few soldiers cheered.

Alysse bit her lip. She didn't like this.

The young man's eyes reflected fear. "I—," he started. "You southerners are barbaric indeed."

"I would not insult the one who holds your life in his hands!" Journande shouted.

There were a few more cheers.

The young man took on a demure stature and breathed, "All right."

The doors of the inner keep opened. The young man was followed by a group composed of men and women in white satin— obviously the Wildsabers. Most had the brown hair, dark eyes, and olive complexion of Kenna. Those that did not were probably married-in— Trowfells, Silverbacks, or others of a lowly house, Alysse reflected.

"I am steward of the keep in the absence of my father," the young man said, his voice assertive despite its shaking. "What are your terms?"

Jourmande removed his greathelm with one hand while his other shook off his blood-drenched sword. "You are hereby stripped of your noble titles," he said. "Furthermore, please step out of the keep and into the city proper."

Reluctantly they walked out of the safety of the keep. Now surrounded, a few of the women began to sniffle.

"Tell me, sir," Jourmande said, looking at the young man with eyes so bloodthirsty it frightened Alysse. "Why would I let a possible contender to the throne live? You have ten seconds to convince me not to burn all of you at the stake."

"*Jourmande!*" Alysse hissed. Then her eyes welled up. She had no power over Jourmande, though he owed everything to her.

"I… I can find you an army!" the young man stammered. "I can convince my father to join you! I can… uhm…"

Jourmande smiled. "I will not burn you at the stake."

The young man sighed in relief.

"I will flog you, and then burn you at the stake!" Jourmande laughed.

Alysse hid her eyes from the horrid sight. It was a grave error. Not only had Jourmande massacred innocents, he had done it with brutality and without respect for Badelgard's laws. Even worse, the people would blame Alysse for it all; she had transported them here. She would bear the responsibility in their eyes. None of them would accept her apology. None would know she had miscalculated, that she had underestimated Jourmande's brutality.

Ever since the ordeal with Kenna, Alysse had wanted the House of Wildsaber to be extinguished; but now she had second thoughts. She regretted leaving Zarubain; she regretted it all as the screams of the Wildsabers reached her.

The soldiers were beating them hard with clubs as they lay there, helpless to the torture. Other soldiers began the construction of wooden pyres. Alysse hid her face and for once wished she stayed in Zarubain. She had brought them here for the good of Badelgard, but none would know it.

She ran away as the soldiers tied up the beaten, bruised nobles; but even outside the walls, she could hear the roar of the ignited fires; she could hear the Wildsabers' first anguished screams.

Gods knew what Jourmande would do next. He would hack and burn through Badelgard, and none could stand against him.

CHAPTER FOURTEEN: SIGMUND BLACKHELM

After the battle, Sigmund rode back with his retinue. He stationed the army in Oskir to further cement his control. Then he locked himself up inside the castle and ordered many kegs of mead and many haunches of lamb and enough salted pork to last him through the summer. If he stayed inside the Golden House and never left, then no assassins could pick him off in the street.

Inside the throne room, he devoured salty pork and guzzled down mead. Lady Kenna watched him with her ghostly brown eyes, peering at him intensely as scraps of meat fell into his beard. Sigmund shivered.

Then Aron, in his short-sleeved blue kirtle, arrived like a ray of sunshine on a cloudy day. "Greetings, Your Majesty," he said, and bowed deeply.

"Do not bow so low," Sigmund said, smiling. "You are the apple of the king's eye, and you should bow only slightly. You may be lowborn, but you are the king's housecarl; and you must never forget it."

"Thank you, Your Majesty," Aron said. His cheeks turned rosy, and he eyed the floor.

Kenna walked off, leaving into the west wing of the Golden House. Sigmund sighed in relief, and uttered a whispered thank-you to the gods.

"Tell me, my valkyrie," Sigmund said, "have you followed up on your little mission?" Five of the Royal Guard stood there with their gold-colored helmets and long spears. Sigmund waved them off. They were sworn to silence and utter loyalty, but he did not like to take chances.

Once the last of the Royal Guard had gone away, Aron walked up to him and said in a low voice, "I have. And she is a witch, truly. And not only a witch, but a dark witch... a witch that has the aid of demons."

Sigmund's neck hairs stood on end, and a chill passed over him. "She must be killed," he said. "You have done well, little Aron."

Aron's cheeks flushed rosy again. "Thank you, master."

How I like it when he calls me 'master,' he reflected again. "Would you like to do the deed, Aron? A knife in the dark? Or, in your case—" He eyed the blade hanging from Aron's belt. "—a sword in the night."

"Do you wish it of me, master?" Aron said. "Whatever you wish, I will do."

"I wish it, but only if you are feeling brave," Sigmund said. "I do not want to lose you, my pet."

"I am brave. I will be brave for you, master."

Sigmund smiled and ran a hand through his glorious blond hair. "Be wise, and be discreet. I do not wish to lose you."

Late that evening, a messenger bolted into the throne room of the Golden House. "Milord. Lady Alysse and her foreign army have laid siege to Wildsaber Keep. They have broken in, and the foreigners are vicious. I fear they may kill everyone there."

Sigmund clutched his heart.

Lady Kenna gave a wild cry. "We must *kill* that southern hussy! Send her to the torturers, and then roast her over a slow flame! I cannot wait to hear her screams…"

Sigmund looked at Kenna with a raised brow. Surely, Alysse would die; yet Kenna's thirst for her blood was unbecoming of a highborn lady. "We must outfit every citizen with weapons. Our veteran soldiers are few, now. But we must fight them…"

"They are knights from the south, milord," the messenger said. "The worst of them have steel mail; the best of them have thick plated armor unlike any of the Badelgarders. We must surrender."

"Surrender?" Sigmund screamed. "Tell me, are you highborn or low?"

The messenger began to quiver. "I am highborn, Your Majesty.

Half Summerleaf, half Silverback."

"Then we will not torture you for demanding that the king surrender." Sigmund stood up and pointed to him. "Guards, kill the coward!"

The messenger screamed and ran for the door. But a pair of Royal Guards blocked him from opening it and cast him to the floor. Sigmund smiled as the blood was shed, as the swords and spears pierced him.

Kenna howled with laughter.

In the early hours of the morning, Sigmund awoke to someone shaking him. Aron stood there in his nightclothes. "Master," he said, "Kenna has discovered me."

After the disorientation left him, Sigmund sat up and snarled, "What do you mean?"

"I mean, master, that I tried to stab her with my sword... but before I landed the blow, she awoke."

"What do you mean?" Sigmund snarled again. "And when she awoke, why did you not finish the deed?"

"Because I looked into her eyes... and I couldn't kill her!"

"You coward! You snake!" Sigmund roared. He grabbed Aron's neck and throttled him. "You beardless boy—nay! You are not a boy at all. You are not even a Badelgarder." He cast him against the wall, and Aron gasped.

"I'm sorry, master."

Sigmund got out of bed and stalked toward Aron. "I will slowly rip the flesh from your bones. Go back and kill her—"

"She's already awake."

The pressure building in Sigmund's chest reached a climax, and then eased. "Aron, I will not let them kill you," he finally said, and smiled at him. "I could not let harm come to my favorite housecarl." He sighed. "Though I regret it, we must not kill Kenna in secret. We must do it in public, and indeed, make it a show."

A smile crept over Aron's face—the same kind of smile that Sigmund wore when he watched torturers kill a lowborn.

CHAPTER FIFTEEN: KAI RIVERHALL

The troll was huge, perhaps twelve feet tall, and covered in black scales. Its eyes were yellow like that of their Ulfr masters, but they glowed like lamps in the deep, skeletal sockets. The troll's teeth were as thin as needles, yet as numerous as strands of hay in a haystack. It was hard to tell where its huge, slovenly head ended and the chest began, but the white, un-scaled chest seemed to be the weakness. It was there where Kai focused.

The troll ran, swift as a bear despite its lumbering steps. It reached back a titanic arm and backhanded Kai. The howling winds knocked the boy hard onto the ice and the troll's slap missed him.

The huge creature leapt into the air.

The shadow of the troll grew larger in size; the monster was intending to crush him with a belly-flop. The troll must weigh a thousand pounds. It would flatten him to paper.

The troll was within mere inches of crushing him when Kai screamed, "*Miuru!*"

The beast howled as it soared backward, as if struck by a fist, and landed on its back in an explosion of ice. In the process of climbing to his feet, Kai slipped several times. He looked at the hulking thing as it lay there.

"Good work," Leif said. "Though you have wasted that word, and its power will not return to you until the morning."

Kai's heart felt tight as it pounded in his chest. "I have wasted it. But I also saved my life... I can fight another day."

"The powers of logomancy—the wizardry of words—is a rare gift," Leif said. "But for reasons unknown, Cani Orion was granted it."

"I am not Cani," Kai said, "so why can I use his power?"

"The Dragon's-Son is a receptacle of power. You absorb whatever magic enters you," Leif said. "The gift of Fire and Salt is already in your bones. But you are a logomancer, too, if you wish to be… The word *miuru* means 'You die!' You must learn more words to fulfill your powers as Dragon's-Son."

"May they only be in the Ulfr tongue?"

"Only in Elvish—the wizards' tongue—or a variety thereof."

"You mean the Ulfr are elves?"

"Calling them elves would be like calling a dog a wolf or a lynx a cat. They have changed much; but I suppose their ancestors were elves." A fire of anger grew in Leif's eyes. "Much has been lost to the human ravaging. My peoples' customs were strange, but we had civilization. You humans burned all our books… destroyed the libraries. Destroyed our learning."

"You speak as if you are one of them."

"I am sorry." Leif patted Kai's back. "I have two natures; sometimes the one I fight gets the best of me."

The winds blew Kai's kirtle about every which way. Snow swirled around him and the howling wind was deafening. His teeth chattered. His ears, long past the painful throes, had turned numb. "We need to go back!" Kai screamed.

"Never!" Leif said. "We must reach the Ulfr rune-stone in the center; there, all the power-words will be yours, and you can put an end to this fell winter."

"I'm going back!" Kai said. A lump of fear grew in his throat; he realized he could not turn back; thanks to the swirling black cloud above him, he could not tell whether he was going west or east, north or south.

"Trust me!" Leif screamed above the deafening wind.

But I do not trust you, Kai thought, *not even after all this.*

A pair of glowing blue eyes appeared in the shadowy blackness that surrounded them. A snarl echoed through the black-clouded endless night: a snarl loud enough to penetrate the shrieking wind. Leif whimpered.

Kai removed his hands from the sleeves of his cloak and drew his ice-cold sword. *This is the end. This is it.*

No sooner had the blue eyes appeared than they vanished into the blackness.

"By Vana," Kai said, "I think we're surrounded."

"Do not say the goddess's name. *I told you that!*" Leif hissed.

Kai followed his guide for an hour more. Then yellow eyes appeared around them: a group of trolls. Aware of his coming death, Kai counted them. One... two...

In all, ten trolls surrounded them. If Kai could not defeat a single troll on his own without a word of power, then there was no chance in all Varda, and in heaven and hell, and in the entire universe, that he could survive them.

"Here is Kai, Dragon's Son," Leif said.

Not in a hundred years did Kai think trolls could talk. The legends said they were dumb as animals.

"Blessed by the Dragon," Leif chanted. "Receptacle of power."

"Stop it!" Kai screamed. "You're frightening me."

"You are a dead man, also," Leif said. "Only a fool would trust an Ulfr!"

Had he truly lied about everything? Had he betrayed him? It was so unlikely. Why, if he betrayed him, had all his explanations about the Words of Power seemed so accurate? Nonetheless, he knew the truth now. Leif had betrayed him.

Kai shrieked in rage, pitched back his saber, and charged Leif. Leif turned and ran away, bounding off like a deer into the darkness with a staff perched nimbly in his fingers.

"Kill him!" Leif's voice carried through the night air.

Kai ran with the speed of the Dragon, but he slipped and fell. The trolls were circling around him. An angry fire grew in Kai—a fire born of light and salt, of green scales. He began to shake at the injustice of it.

He was about to charge into the darkness when a troll ran at him, tearing across the ice on all fours. But Kai was not himself. His blood burned with anger. The only emotion he felt was rage; there was no fear in him, anymore.

The troll's hand slammed into his back, but his spine did not shatter nor did his skin break. Elastically, he withstood the blow. Another slap hit him from the opposite direction, striking his jaw. There was a brief pain, but his teeth neither fell out nor came loose.

Kai grappled the troll. They gripped each other's hands: Kai, a young man of less than a hundred-and-fifty pounds, versus a behemoth that weighed probably ten times the amount. He did not think of it that way; this huge hulk was blocking him from his goal: killing Leif.

In the end the troll was forced to stumble backward, falling flat on its ridged spine. Kai turned to run where Leif had gone, and another troll blocked his path. This one was larger than the last—a giant behemoth of blackish-purple scales and huge, hate-filled eyes.

It let out a deafening roar that overtook Kai's world and eviscerated his senses. Green phlegm landed in Kai's face and eyes, and the gaping mouth was large enough to swallow a horse whole, but it only made Kai angrier. Kai let out a roar of his own—not as loud as the troll's, but as it continued, it was louder than Kai ever screamed before.

Kai threw his sword into the gaping black maw. Instantly, the troll's scream stopped. The blade went down into his throat, doubtlessly cutting up its innards. Kai laughed. He'd never get the saber back—the weapon he'd had since his coming-of-age.

The trolls looked skittish now. As Kai searched for Leif through the swirling gray snow, he came to the realization that his betrayer was long gone. And then—as his angry shaking faded—all his energy vanished. He collapsed to the ice, hitting his head hard, and blacked out in the twisting darkness.

CHAPTER SIXTEEN: ALYSSE RIVERHALL

It was a sight Alysse would never forget. Towering flames consumed the buildings of Wildsaber Keep, and the outer walls had begun to smoke. Thanks to the flammable items inside, even the stone-walled inner keep appeared to be burning. Ravens circled overhead, as if mourning the death of their home. For a brief moment, Alysse mourned with them.

Within the raging inferno, the bodies of the dead piled higher than the walls and roasted along with the buildings. Alysse never wanted to know the smell of burning human flesh, but now she did. It sickened her.

All through it, she watched, realizing she had no choice but to follow Sir Jourmande. Without his protection, the nobles of Badelgard would capture and kill her. Bringing a foreign army into the homeland was an unforgiveable transgression; and if her heart turned homeward, she would never be welcome in Voraigne Manor again.

They rode hard, going east. In time, the Waterwood vanished behind them. The land began a steady upward ascent, and the sides of the river valley grew rockier. Soon, sheer cliff-faces appeared. In time the valley would become an impassible canyon, with the Great Falls gushing down to the bottom and the kingly city of Oskir at the top, impossible to scale.

They set up camp along the shore of the river. They made campfires in the chilly evening, not without struggle.

It's summer, by the gods, Alysse thought. *It should not be this cold.*

Sir Jourmande sat next to her at the same fire, though not on purpose. Alysse had ridden in the vanguard with him, and the only space left was next to her. No one wanted to sit with her, the ignoble, ambitious woman whom Jourmande had made a fool of.

"We must scale the valley while we have the chance," Alysse told Jourmande but not daring to look him in the eyes.

"If you think I'm going to take commands from a whore, you are mistaken," Jourmande said. "Your child did not belong to your former husband. You should not be allowed to speak in public."

That was simply uncalled-for.

Tears formed in Alysse's eyes, but she pretended that she heard nothing.

By late afternoon of the next day, the sides of the river valley had become sheer rock cliffs. Jourmande realized that Alysse was right. The way to Oskir was not directly east.

With a reluctant command by Jourmande, the army turned around, pressing westward as quickly as they could. But they were not fast enough. Clouds formed overhead and a light drizzle began. The piney wood became dead silent. The winds were blowing purple thunderheads in from the west. A storm was coming.

"Take shelter!" Jourmande shouted. "Set up the tents at once!"

The army scrambled to obey his command, but they weren't fast enough. The winds howled and the rain pelted Alysse. The wetness and cold caused both of them to shiver.

A crow flew down onto a pine bough. It was huge, even for a crow, and its feathers wide as gardening-spades. Its eyes were black and beady, as any other of its kind, but somehow reflected intelligence.

A blue flash of lightning lit up the western sky, illuminating an army. They were not darklings—Alysse could tell from the rosy color in their stern, somber faces—but they were not human, either. Their shields bore the sign of a skull. They wore no armor. Their ears were long and pointed. Their irises were yellow, and their skin almost as hairy as a bear's. They were singing in a strange tongue.

These were Ulfr. Alysse had heard legends about them, but never in a thousand years did she think she would see them in the flesh.

"To arms!" Jourmande screamed, and drew his sword. He had already put aside his armor. He grabbed his helmet and put it on; he looked naked, now, with just a thin shirt and a pair of loose woolen breeches. Yet now Alysse could see and—despite herself—admire the iron thews of his arms and calves. Sir Jourmande was a heartless man, a brutal man... but he was a strong, formidable warrior, and fair of form.

"To arms!" Jourmande repeated at a scream. His underlings scrambled to obey his command.

Then—of all things—the crow spoke. "Darklings are easy foes. They are nothing more than humans raised to un-death. We—the mighty Sorelden—are returned from our dark cairns. Without the power of the Green Dragon, you humans are hopeless against us. And all will fall."

A bowstring twanged. An arrow from a soldier struck the bird, piercing through its thin chest. It fell from the pine bough and landed on the ground. It fluttered for a while, but then its feathers molted, and it grew simultaneously larger and longer until it had taken the shape of one of the Ulfr.

His ears were long. His eyes were yellow. He looked no different from the other Ulfr, except for the tattered purple cloak he wore. The arrow had fallen away from him.

Alysse had never seen anyone shift from a form to another. She had only heard about it in stories.

"My name is Cani Orion!" the Ulfr leader shouted. "I am a wizard of the ninth degree, and *kinthir*."

Jourmande heaved back his sword.

"I would not test me."

Jourmande rushed him.

"*Tiornu!*" Cani shouted.

Suddenly Jourmande fell forward on his face, as stiffly as an ice statue.

"I will let you eat worms for a while," Cani said. He pointed to

Sir Gorbande—youngest of the knights—and cried, *"Miuru!"*

Sir Gorbande exploded. Bits of flesh flew everywhere, leaving only bone. His skeleton collapsed to the ground. Blood pelted Alysse's face and stained her dress.

She thought of running, but did not want to draw the attention of this demon.

Cani smiled darkly. "We can be enemies, or we can be friends… what is your name?"

"Jourmande," he wheezed.

"My mission is simple," Cani said. "You must split up into seven groups and go to the seven keeps of Badelgard. You must find a boy named Kai Riverhall… and you must knife him to death in his sleep."

Kai Riverhall, Alysse thought. *I do not recognize that name. Yet he is a Riverhall; I would never harm him.*

"If you do not find him," Cani said, "I will kill all of you." He flicked his hands—which, Alysse noticed, only had three fingers and a thumb—and Jourmande's stiff body relaxed.

After some heavy breathing, he struggled to his feet and stumbled forward dizzily. He still clutched his sword in his right hand. "Damn these eyes! My vision is blurred, but I swear you are a bear fit for slaying."

"In the Sorelden tongue, 'Cani' means bear," he said. "And a bear I will be, if you do not obey my commands."

Jourmande screamed, "For Lady Marabelle!" and charged Cani. But honor—Alysse reflected—would get him nowhere in this situation. The horse goddess would not ride out of heaven to protect her champion. That only happened in songs.

"Tiornu!" Cani shouted, and Jourmande fell rigidly again, straight onto his face. "You do not learn your lessons well, do you?"

If only Alysse had learned the craft of healing from the priestesses of Vana, she might be able to counteract the wizard's devilry.

"Will you listen to me now?" Cani said.

"Speak to me!" Alysse shouted. "I am a true Badelgader.

According to honor, I should be commanding the army. Not this man here."

Cani's eyes met hers, and how they unsettled her—bright, yellow, glittering. "Human woman," he said. "I could make an example of you, too."

"Hear me, sir," Alysse said calmly but firmly. Indeed, she could end up like Sir Gorbande if she didn't act wisely. "I beg you to release him."

"Release him?" Cani looked at her with curious eyes and cocked his head. The black hair that covered his body made him look like a beast rather than a sentient creature. "Why would I release him, pretty woman? Tell me, pretty woman with hairless skin. With fair eyes of green. With healthy, red lips?"

The thought of Cani as a mate was unthinkable, like bedding a goat or a horse. "You should release him," Alysse said, stumbling over her words. She had walked into a tangled web of her own creation. "Because…"

Cani bared his fangs. A low growl emitted from his throat.

"Because—" Alysse, foreseeing an imminent death, thought of what the Voraignese loved the most. "—because by King and Country, and by Greatshadowed Umbra, and for the life of bloody *Jourmande*… CHARGE!"

The pounding of hooves filled Alysse's ears. She dove as Cani pointed at her and shouted a word of death. As she leapt, the ground around her wavered like it did during a heat wave in Zarubain, and there was a deafening boom.

She looked down at her body. It was still intact. His dark magic had missed her.

Facing the feather-plumed, helmeted giants that were the Knights of Marabelle, Alysse saw a trace of fear in some of the Ulfr's shifty yellow eyes.

There were more deaths—knights exploding in their armor, and footmen shedding their flesh—but there were almost eight thousand members of the army.

Just minutes into the conflict, a huge, black-feathered crow arose from the raging army and flew off west toward the sun. The Ulfr soon lay dead.

Alysse laughed. As she looked into the soldiers' eyes—for the first time in her entire life—she saw respect.

CHAPTER SEVENTEEN: SIGMUND BLACKHELM

When the early morning darkness fled, and the sun arose over the eastern farmers' fields, King Sigmund ordered for the arrest of Kenna Wildsaber. Yet when the Royal Guard, accompanied by Sigmund, searched her room, she was gone. She had left her wardrobe, her books of sorcery, and—most notably—her girls, behind.

Sir Aron's assassination attempt had scared her, apparently.

"We must put her name on the Hangman's List," Sigmund said.

The Royal Guards watched in silence, yet Sigmund could see the judgment in their eyes.

"Am I not king?" he roared, and grabbed a guard by his Blackhelm surcoat. "Are my pronouncements not law? If I say we must put someone on the Hangman's List, then it must be done. It does not matter who it is, lowborn or high."

"They will obey," Sir Aron said. "I will see to it."

"Good," Sigmund roared. "Make sure it is done, Aron, and tell the Ears of the Realm to search for her far and wide. She must be brought back to answer for her witchcraft."

That afternoon, a messenger arrived in the throne room.

"My king," he said, "the army of Alysse advances. They are nearly upon our doorstep."

"Grab him!" Sigmund shouted.

The Royal Guards fell upon him, took his quivering form into their iron-lined hands.

"Don't kill me!" the man cried. "I am just a messenger... I did not cause Alysse to attack you, my king. I am your loyal subject. I support your rule to the fullest!"

"Your toadying words do not affect me at all," Sigmund hissed. "You are a sniveling wretch. Tell me, are you lowborn or high?"

"Low, my lord," the man said, "and I look upon the High as gods."

Sigmund balled his fists and stood up. "Alas for you, wretch!" He grunted, and saw this man for what he was—pathetic. "Give him a good flogging, and give him the thumbscrew. When his cries are enough for you, kill him."

"No! No, please!" the messenger cried as the guards dragged him out of the throne room. "Please, no, Your Worship!"

Yet only seconds after he left, Sigmund's mind began to race. He wondered if he had made a mistake. He wondered if he shouldn't have killed the man; if he should have let the wretch live.

Perhaps he was not a traitor. Not everyone is against me.

Sir Aron entered through a side door.

Sir Aron is not against me. Sigmund smiled.

"I have found Lady Kenna," said the young man.

"Thank the gods!" Relief washed through Sigmund's body, loosening tense muscles and warming him. "You have done well. Where is she?"

"She is at the smithy, sir. Hennard's smithy, in a black cloak to hide her face."

"You have done well."

"I suggest you come alone," Sir Aron said. "She is watchful, and if she sees any but you coming, then she will surely run away."

"Run?" Sigmund said. "I will order the gates shut. She will not escape."

"Milord," Sir Aron said, and a hint of irritation laced his voice. "We must hurry. There is no time to shut the gate, or make any preparations. Come with me, and fast!"

Sigmund nodded and ran with Aron, spurred on by the urgency

in his voice. Sigmund was a big man—and a fat man, too—but he had been trained in the sword by the greatest of teachers.

Indeed, a woman in a black cloak waited at the blacksmith. She was the height and shape of Lady Kenna. Hennard, the old lowborn forger of horseshoes and various knickknacks, stood with her. His old, brown-gray beard hung to his knees, forked and braided. His eyes looked on Sigmund with unacceptable derision.

"You are under arrest. You are a witch, and witches must be burned. Hennard will burn with you, for he has harbored you." Sigmund drew his sword. "Sir Aron, bind her and take her back to the Golden House." He smiled, feeling satisfied that he had caught the prize and soon the smoke of her burning would waft into the sky like a sacrifice.

"I don't want to."

Sigmund looked back. Surely Sir Aron had not said those words. Yet the young man looked at him with an expression he had never seen before: narrowed eyes, pursed lips—a sneer.

"What do you mean, my valkyrie?" Sigmund said. "You must obey me, for you are my housecarl. And you are my friend."

Sir Aron howled with laughter and swept his sword from its scabbard. "Time to fight, fattykins! You think you can contend with me, pork-belly? Come on! Prove your worth, you sad excuse for a king."

"What are you saying?" Gooseflesh spread over Sigmund's body.

Kenna lowered her hood, and a smile was on her face.

"No! No…"

Sir Aron smiled, and it was a smile Sigmund recognized in himself. Pleasure in the pain of others: Sadism. Sigmund turned to run but the people—the dirty commoners in their dull brown clothing—surrounded him, blocking his way.

"I hate you," Sir Aron said. "You disgust me. You're fat, incompetent, and paranoid, and I always thought you were lower than a worm. I never liked you, not once during my tenure as housecarl."

"My valkyrie… you break my heart." Tears formed in his eyes.

Sir Aron howled with laughter. The common people followed, and Sigmund flushed hot in embarrassment.

"You're pathetic." Sir Aron chuckled. "You murder, and you torture, but you are not really a man. King Sven was twice the man you were, and Sven was a worm as well."

"My valkyrie!" Sigmund shrieked. "My valkyrie!"

Sir Aron dashed toward him; Sigmund parried, but with a flick of the wrist Aron disarmed him. The sword hit the dirt. With two quick cuts, Sir Aron slashed open wounds on both Sigmund's cheeks, and then he kicked him to the ground.

"Strike him the death-blow," Kenna said. "Make it quick."

"He is a worm." Sigmund tried to sit up but Aron slammed down the heel of his boot and forced him back down. "Worms," he continued, "must be made to suffer a bit."

The lowborns around Sigmund cheered. Tears streaked from his eyes, running down his ears. He trembled as he lay there. Blood collected from his cheek-wounds. Sir Aron's smile had grown, and now Sigmund could see both white rows of teeth.

"*Make him suffer!*" cried a tall man in the crowd. "*Make him suffer like we suffered!*"

"No—" Sigmund started but Aron slammed his boot down again and his ribs shuddered.

"Do not talk, worm." Aron spat on him. "You are not a man, but a pig. So squeal."

Sigmund drew in a phlegmy breath. He coughed. "Please!"

Aron's eyes blazed. "*Squeal!*" He slammed his boot down on Sigmund and a few ribs cracked, sending throes of pain through his body.

Sigmund screamed.

"Good! Now *squeal. Squeal again,* piggy!"

Sigmund squealed, but it apparently did not satisfy Aron; the boot slammed down again into his heart, and pain exploded through him. He wept.

"*Squeal! Squeal! Squeal!*"

Sigmund choked on his tears, and the coughing caused almost more pain than Aron's constant kicks. All the while, the people cheered. Through weary eyes, Sigmund could see Kenna smiling brightly.

Forgive me, Vana, for my crimes, and take me into your home. Yet the good goddess would never accept someone like Sigmund into her presence.

"Alas," Sir Aron said. "Though the pig squeals, he does not satisfy me. He must be punished!"

Sigmund groaned. His body ached, and nausea settled over him.

"Bring me a ladle of molten copper," Sir Aron said.

"Sir..." Hennard looked at him with a furrowed brow.

Even the crowd looked at him with raised brows and uncertain expressions.

"*Do it!*" Kenna howled. "You heard the housecarl. I am next in line to the throne, and I demand you listen."

Sigmund shut his eyes, savoring his last minutes before the terror. It seemed hardly a second before Sir Aron tore his eyes open and forced him to view the ladle of molten copper pouring down toward his throat.

CHAPTER EIGHTEEN: KAI RIVERHALL

When Kai awoke, he sensed he was not in the snowy hell of the Ice Shelf. Yet he could hear the endless wind and feel the dead air in his mind. Only after severe denial did he realize he was in a house, in a room overlooking a piney meadow, and resting in complete silence. A bowl of boiled vegetables sat next to him. So did a woman.

She had long brown hair, streaked with gold, which fell to the floor. She sat in a chair.

"Where am I? Where's... Leif?" Kai didn't know why he asked that question. The grievances of the past were long gone, and he should be thankful that he was alive.

"Leif is close-by," the woman answered.

"What do you mean?" Kai snapped. "Surely..." He gasped for breath. "What's your name?"

"I go by Nessa when I am here, in this land." She had a strange accent. "My true name is Gudrun."

"You say Leif is close. Therefore, I you must serve the enemy... Cani Orion and the trolls."

"There is worse to fear than Cani Orion. Compared to the Great Witch, he is an ant to be crushed. And when the Seat of the Mother is fully pulled out of the ice, she will be invincible." Gudrun's expression turned motherly, at which Kai bristled with irritation. "Now finish your soup," she said. "Eat the vegetables or you'll never return to good health."

Kai's muscles were jelly. He tried to lift his arms, but they seemed in open rebellion against him; they would not respond. "Why am I so weak?"

"The dragon's strength was so powerful that, when he left you, your own strength left." She spoon-fed him some boiled carrots. They were horribly unsalted, tasteless as water.

"You didn't answer my other question," Kai said. "Are you friends with Leif?"

"I am Leif," Gudrun said.

"What?" Kai spat the carrots from his mouth. "What in Varda are you talking about?"

"I am Firstborn of the goddess Vana. I am the Guardian of Altgard. I am Gudrun, Queen of the Valkyries."

I'm lodging with a madwoman. "First you're Leif," Kai said. "Then you're a valkyrie. I wonder what you will be next."

"Leif Helgursson does not exist," Gudrun said. "He is a figment of my imagination. Bodily possession is within the power of valkyries."

"Spread your wings and fly, and bring me back a tuft of cloud. Then we'll talk."

"I would not make such a grand display of my power without necessity," Gudrun said. "Besides, in this form I can neither fly nor wield the lightning spear. You saved your own life on the Ice Shelf; I merely dragged you to safety."

"So you are a valkyrie, but you can neither fly nor kill," Kai said. "Have you ever considered the possibility that you might be just touched in the head?"

Gudrun struck him in the jaw. It hurt; she was strong. "Do not speak to a daughter of Vana that way. And do not speak about the touched in that way, either, for they are already troubled."

"I am sorry." His jaw throbbed where she had struck him.

"I control this body like I controlled Leif's," Gudrun said. "Her—my!—name was Nessa, and she was a lowborn spinner of wool. She had a secret, though; she was an oracle gifted with far-sight. She prayed fervently every day that the gods would use her as an instrument against the coming evil—the encroaching darkness she saw so clearly in her mind. She got her wish when an Ulfr struck her down with a sword. By Vana's grace, they did not bewitch her into a darkling. Her body lay still only an hour before I disposed of Leif and took on her form. In the end, her dying wish was fulfilled."

"What a good woman," Kai said. "Was she married?"

"No," Gudrun answered. "Nessa never married. She was thirty years old and never knew love."

Over the next week, Gudrun sang Kai songs. Her voice was strong and pure. It reverberated through the small house, and Kai suspected it was aiding his recovery. Little by little, Kai regained the ability to sit up and feed himself.

One morning, Kai stood up onto his feet. The weight of his body was crushing under his atrophied legs, but he managed to stumble out of his chamber and into the small common room, where Gudrun sat relaxed.

Kai fell onto a chair.

"You look well," Gudrun said.

"Is what you said when you were Leif true? That I am the Dragon's-Son? That I am blessed by Skruga?"

"It is all true," Gudrun said. "The reason I betrayed you as Leif was for your own good; your anger gave you the strength of the Dragon."

"Wise." Kai reflected on what all had gone on. A troll—a *bloody* troll—crushed him with both hands, and he survived. "What now?" he said. "We don't have the Ulfr runestone, so I don't know any more Words of Power."

Gudrun wore an expression of similar frustration. "Unfortunately, I do not know much more of the language beyond what Cani Orion has said."

Suddenly Kai had an idea. "I know," he said. "I will go to Oskir."

"Why to the City of Kings?" Gudrun said, looking baffled. "People leave the city every day; they can see the storm-clouds coming. King Sigmund died and armies gather to take the throne..."

"Truly?" Kai said.

Gudrun nodded. "It would be most unwise to visit the City of

Kings at such a dark hour."

"Unwise, but it is the only option," Kai said. "In the City of Kings, inside the Golden House, there's an Ulfr lexicon. It has all the ancient Ulfr words, and the direct translation!" He had tried to convince Master Frey to let him find it, albeit for different reasons.

Gudrun's eyes widened. "You're right. One of the few books you Badelgarders possess… I had forgotten."

"I didn't know valkyries forgot things."

"In this mortal frame, my mind is deteriorated," Gudrun said, "as is my strength and my swiftness. In Altgard, I am the strongest of all my sisters… and the highest of the flyers. Here, in this body, I am weak."

Kai put a reassuring hand on her shoulder. For a second he caught a whiff of rot; Gudrun's possessed body had, after all, lain in death for a while. It was a faint smell, though, so very faint. He wondered whether valkyries took lovers, and what the love of valkyries would be like. Yet the woman before him was not a white-winged, spear-wielding Daughter of Vana, but instead the mind and soul of a valkyrie inside an aging lowborn woman. It was the soul that mattered, though—the mind, not the body.

"If we go to Oskir, we must move swiftly," Gudrun said.

"You're right," Kai said. "We must pack every bit of food there is…"

"I checked the larder. There is only stale bread. We used everything; we may have to go hungry on our journey."

Kai sighed in disappointment. "Pack the stale bread, just in case. I still have my bow, I assume."

Gudrun nodded.

"I will hunt and forage as needed."

Gudrun smiled. "I am glad the Dragon's-Son is a Scout of Woodhome, and not a loafer from Andarr's Port."

They set off the next morning. Kai's stomach growled as he

walked through the snow—and gods knew what he would give for a roast boar—but his eyes looked only ahead. Gudrun—or should he say, Nessa—stumbled behind him; apparently it took a long time to get used to a new body.

Yet Kai knew what lay ahead of him. A proud city, an old city, half as large as Andarr's Port but twice as honorable. A city without a ruler, a flock without a shepherd: Oskir, City of Kings.

CHAPTER NINETEEN: ALYSSE RIVERHALL

The army had lost three knights and twenty men to the wizard's spells. In all they were in good shape. Their commander, however, was not. Sir Jourmande lay still, unmoving and unspeaking. Were his eyes not open and his chest heaving with breath, Alysse would think him dead.

"Who shall lead now?" said Sir Cherbot, a huge, black-moustached man who was more fat than muscle. "Our great commander is dead, and to be honest, I would take no orders from any of you jelly-livered louts."

"And I would never take commands from you!" cried the long-haired, and according to some, effeminate, knight Sir Logrin. "You truly should lay off the fish jellies and Potatoes Garronais. It's a miracle you can fight, with all that extra baggage hanging from your gullet!"

"Whatever you say, fair maiden," Cherbot sneered. "Don't forget to clean the house when you get home."

"Is that the best you can do?" Sir Logrin laughed.

"Listen to me!" Alysse shouted at the top of her lungs. "I will lead you! I am the Daughter Vis Voraigne! I am a competent commander! And braver than any man I know!"

"You are the belle of the army—the apple of our eyes," Cherbot said. "Bed me, wench, over and over, and I'll follow you as long as you keep me company."

I'd rather bed an Ulfr. Alysse managed not to say that, though the thought was true.

"Why don't we heal him?" said brown-haired, unkempt Sir Visseau. "Surely the thought has occurred to you, Cherbot Bricks-for-Brains and weak-kneed Logrin."

Alysse cried, "Listen to me!" But she knew they would never listen to her. She was a woman. Without a strong-armed man like Jourmande, she was nothing. The Zarubes might elevate women to high stature in courtly poetry…but they are only prizes to be won—never the equals of men.

"We will take our respective soldiers," Logrin said. "We will divvy up this barren land and form petty kingdoms. We will all compromise. Every Knight of Marabelle will be a king."

"May hells take you, Logrin!" Alysse shouted. But she was invisible and inaudible. They ignored her as if she were just a cricket chirping, a whispering of the wind.

Filled with despair, she ran into the Journmande's old tent, where his—or more accurately, Alysse's—stores of gold were waiting.

She filled every pocket, every fold of her dress, with gold. She removed everything unnecessary from her pack and filled it to the brim with gold. With this money, she could afford to begin a new life. In some distant country, in some barren, backward land, she would live out her life. She would not be noble because none would believe she was the Daughter Vis Voraigne. Her dress was in tatters—not fitting for a noblewoman—and her father would not vouch for her.

When she left the tent, Sir Logrin was smothering Sir Journmande with a pillow.

Alysse spoke with calm indifference. "What are you doing?"

"We have voted," Sir Logrin said. "We know our lord, and he would rather die than be seen in such a pathetic state."

"Ah," Alysse said with equal indifference, realizing that she did not truly care. After how Sir Journmande treated her, she did not care whether he lived or died.

In time Journmande stopped breathing.

Alysse realized that Sir Cherbot and Sir Visseau were gone. "Where are—?"

Sir Logrin stood up from his dark deed and looked at her, smiling. His teeth were pure white, obviously either cleaned thoroughly with powder or bleached. His skin was smooth and unblemished, save a small scar running across his cheek. Most would find his face comely, yet it was a beauty borne of effeminacy and immaculate care, and Alysse—a Badelgarder through-and-through—did not find such a beauty attractive in the slightest.

"Cherbot has taken his two hundred men. Visseau has taken his three hundred," Logrin said. "Sir Lirac and Sir Carbidonne have gone as well. Those few dozen who remain are taking their soldiers, and we will divvy up the land as I said."

Alysse sneered. "And what parcel of land will you take, 'Sir' Logrin?"

"I will take Oskir, City of Kings," the knight answered. "Five-hundred men are under my command, the most of any Knight of Marabelle. And by the horse goddess—by her silver mane—I will be the greatest of the knight-kings."

"Will you marry me, then? May I be your queen?" Alysse said. It was worth a try.

Logrin threw back his head and laughed. His blond hair shimmered in the gray, cloudy light. "Jourmande has told me about you, and it is not good. Your child—gods grant him rest—

did not belong to your husband. You, dearest, Alysse, are mistaken if you think I will wed a common whore."

"Umbra beshadow you!" Alysse shrieked. Her eyes welled with tears. "You would not marry a woman anyway, Logrin, for you *are* one."

She ran away, fleeing the vast host.

A few minutes passed. She caught sight—on the grass—a gold coronet. It was the coronet of Andarr's Port. It was belonged to Harald. Harald was nearby. She gasped at this and ascended the valley at a run.

Up on the high plain lay a land of the dead. Monstrous darklings wandered the bleak landscape, growling like angry dogs. Alysse—gods be damned—should have brought a sword. She cursed herself, and then she saw him.

Alysse's long-dead husband was walking toward her. Harald's skin was silver, and his eyes, red. Yet he was still handsome. He could still very well be the idol of the Andarr's Port girls, of the common women who dreamed about him by day and cursed themselves by night. Yet he could never be had... not even by his own wife.

Alysse wept. She walked up to him, tears flowing, and touched his hand. A low, growling sound was issuing from his throat. He stared at her with dead eyes. Alysse, by now in tears, knelt before him and reached for his rope belt. She removed it, and the breeches fell down.

She did her deed.

The unwholesome liquor was frigid from death. She flushed hot. She thought that perhaps he had returned to his normal self; she arose, feeling ashamed, looked into her husband's dead eyes, and kissed his lips.

He bit her.

The light bite did not break skin, and Alysse pushed him away. He was a darkling, through and through. She fell into weeping. She ran away, tears pouring, body shaking.

That night, amid the freezing snow, she collapsed. She lay in the shade of a pine. Seeing Harald had been the only comfort for a long time.

Harald—curse his bones—was a darkling, now. She wept.

Her tears turned to icicles in the wintry air. *Gods be damned, it's summer. It should be* warm!

She needed go back to the lowlands, find shelter. But she, an aristocrat whom servants had helped all her life, could not navigate this treacherous terrain. Exploring and surviving in the wild were the skills of the Scouts of Woodhome, not the bloody Daughter Vis Voraigne.

She stood up in the flurries of snow. She knew the storm would kill her if she did not act. She ran through the snowy hills of the uplands and surveyed the landscape. Before her was a great green expanse. Far to the east lay the great mountains. Somewhere in the west lay Blackhelm

Keep, but she would not be welcomed there. The Priests of the Dragonmount would welcome her, but they had gone to fight trolls in the Ice Shelf. Their stone temple was now empty.

She cried out as the snow whirled around her, suffocating her. Then, in the distance, she spotted smoke.

She ran all the way to the smoke's source, and found a makeshift camp. They were all men and—judging by their chainmail hauberks, iron helmets, and their swords and spears—they were warriors. On their shields was the black-gold eagle of the Blackhelms.

Just her luck; Sigmund Blackhelm was her enemy. But she could not survive this storm. They were her only hope, and capture was something she had to risk.

She ran into the camp and was greeted with drawn swords and confused mutters. "Pardon me!" she said. "I will die in this storm if I don't find warmth."

The captain, carrying a steel spangenhelm in his right hand, made his way through the crowd of spears. "Your honor," he said. "You appear to be a fine lady, judging by your clothes."

Alysse laughed. Her dress, once bright green, was brown and in tatters. The hem was lined with dried mud and several holes marred its once-beautiful appearance. Perhaps the brooch and jewelry that Alysse wore gave the captain that impression. "I am honored to be in your presence, sir."

"Nonsense," the captain said. "Come... take a seat by the fire, and we will bring you some porridge."

"What are you doing in this wild land?" Alysse asked as she ate the porridge, savoring its thickness and richness.

"Sigmund Blackhelm paid us to paint our shields with his Black-and-Gold Eagle," the captain said. "We obeyed. He told us to patrol

Trowheim and protect it from the Osters. Then we heard tell of other things in Badelgard. The dead walking again. An Ulfr witch. And an army of the south arriving on distant shores…"

"Do you still serve Sigmund?" Alysse said.

"Nay," the captain said. "Our allegiance to him can be measured in coin, and now his coin is dried-up. We have already spent all the gold he gave us. It wasn't much, but times are difficult and our savings are little."

Alysse had an idea. "Will you serve me if I pay you?" she said.

"I will serve a *demon* if he pays me," the captain said. "We are mercenaries. We will serve anyone with the proper gold."

"Then I will pay you eight-hundred gold coins to serve me for the next two years. You must paint your shields with the Golden Bear of the Riverhalls," Alysse said. "We will retake Andarr's Port."

"Nay, woman," the captain said. "It would be better to take Oskir."

"The City of Kings is impregnable unless we have southern siege weapons," Alysse argued. "It is built on a hill. And Sigmund Blackhelm has an army to defend it."

"Sigmund Blackhelm is dead," the captain said. "Oskir is at its weakest. It has no leader, and many aspirants claiming the kingship. We are close. And we could pillage—"

"There is to be *no* pillaging," Alysse demanded. "*None.* The entirety of the mission will be to take Oskir… leave the citizens be. And I will be the High Queen of Badelgard."

"I admire your ambition," the captain said, and smiled.

"You are the first man to say as much," Alysse said, and returned his smile. "What is your name?"

"Ivarr son of Ivarr," the captain said. "I am lowborn."

"It matters not whether you are lowborn or highborn," Alysse said. "I have had enough treachery from the highly born anyway. Lords, knights, and earls; they cannot be trusted."

Ivarr's smile grew bigger. "We will serve you gladly. We are three hundred strong, and more skilled than any other."

"Soon Oskir will be ours," Alysse said, "and I will be High Queen of Badelgard."

INTERLUDE II:
SIR ARON SVENSSON

Light dawned over Oskir. The city had no king, but the ordeal with King Sigmund had put Sir Aron into a long afterglow. Aron never had such fun in his life—torturing the sad, pathetic old man and watching the horror in his eyes; seeing him feel betrayed as Aron finally told him how he really felt. Even the citizens thought he had gone overboard, but they weren't going to make Aron feel guilty. Guilt never worked on him.

Aron sat in a chair, looking into Kenna's eyes in the privacy of her bedchamber. He laughed quietly at the thought of pitiful Sigmund. Serious things needed to be discussed, but Aron was still caught up in the rush. He knew he had to do it again; but he could not—after the trust he built up over many months—repeat the thrill very easily.

Then, as he stared into Kenna's eyes, he saw a miserable old shrew who fancied herself a great wizard. "I will be king," he snapped. "I will command Badelgard. I deserve it more than you!"

"You are lowborn," Kenna sneered. "It has been in the law code since the time of the Wardens. Not even a housecarl—if he is lowborn—can be proclaimed King of Badelgard."

"And a woman may never assume the throne, lowborn or high!" Sir Aron hissed. I will be king. You will make me king, or I will kill you, she-wolf. You will marry me. I command it."

Kenna's expression darkened like a coming storm. For a second Aron feared her, but it only lasted a moment; she was a little sniveling shrew, and she would learn to respect him.

"I have power beyond imagining," Kenna boomed. "You are a little beardless boy, and I am a wizard!"

"If you don't shut your mouth, she-wolf, then I'll do to you what I did to Sigmund!" Sir Aron stood up and fumbled over to the nightstand to grab his sword.

Kenna threw her hands forward. Aron hurtled off the bed and hit the wall hard.

"Agh!" He gasped, but there was no air. The blow knocked the wind out of him. Finally he saw her magic; and for once he was afraid. But he wouldn't let the miserable witch get away with it.

"That is just a taste of my power." Kenna's voice boomed like thunder, reverberating through the walls. Her face darkened, and the light of the candles dimmed. "I have the aid of the Black Mist. I have stared into the Abyss, and I have conquered it."

"I said shut your sniveling mouth!" Sir Aron ran at her and in the process grabbed his sword. He leapt on the bed, intending to bounce over it; Kenna threw her hands forth once more and he hit the wall, and the air was sucked out of him again. Yet still he clutched the sword, managing to hold on just barely.

"Try again." Kenna's voice was gravelly, demonic. "I will kill you."

The words only infuriated Aron more. He'd torture the she-wolf, and he'd make it worse than Sigmund. With a cry of rage, he charged again, hacking down with his sword as he finally bounced off the bed toward her; and the blade was an inch from her forehead when suddenly a searing black fire melted the sword like ice tossed into a hearth.

"You will die now!" Kenna's face had turned a shade of red, but it was not anger; it was as if she were half-changed into a demon of hell. Her eyes blazed with fire. "I am granted the power of Baa'oul the Great Slug, who gorges on the damned, and his feast never ends! Lord Baa'oul, I commend this soul to you. Let him not know the light of heaven, but only the burning of your gullet…"

Twin black flames danced in her hands. "Worship me! *Car'norhag shuggoth! Vach! Vach! VACH!*" Green acid spewed from her mouth and melted through Sir Aron's face.

He screamed and went blind.

But despite the blackness—in his mind's eye—he could see

Kenna's face crawling with maggots. A grin went from under her nose to the ends of both her ears. She opened a wide smacking mouth, filled with rotted yellow teeth. She had become the Power that she invoked—Baa'oul, the Great Slug, the Eater of the Damned. She did not serve the Ulfr; she served a demon.

Aron tried to scream but couldn't do it as the foul bile continued melting his skin. The pain was excruciating. He crumpled to his knees.

The last thing he felt was Kenna's teeth sinking into his thigh. She would eat him for the sake of Baa'oul. Aron had never prayed before, but he begged the gods that a demon would never sit upon the High Throne of Badelgard.

CHAPTER TWENTY: KAI RIVERHALL

As Kai and Gudrun traveled to Oskir, news reached them along the roads. Sigmund had died, as had his housecarl. The coronation of Lady Kenna took place just yesterday. Meanwhile, foreign knights divvied up the land between themselves. The Ulfr walked again. Lady Alysse could not be found, and the kingdom lay in turmoil.

"Dark times," Gudrun said, "and only the Dragon's Son can save us."

"It is indeed a dark time if it lies on a person like me to save the world," Kai said. In the distance, the Golden Gate appeared before them as the rushing of King's Falls echoed across the land. "There is Oskir."

"In the time of the founders, the city was much smaller," Gudrun said. "No walls, only a handful of longhouses and huts. And before the founders, the Ulfr dared not build a settlement here. They considered it a sacred place; and an oracle lived here, staring into the waters for answers. The Great Mother aided them with her Evil Eye; and their powers of divination were great. They knew of their coming doom hundreds of years before Buntringer scaled the Sky Cliffs."

"So why did they not prepare?"

"The prophecy of the Green Dragon was hidden from their eyes. They prepared for battle against humans… but against Dragonfire, they had no defense."

They passed through the gates.

The low town looked much the same, and yet the air was different. They took up lodging at the inn (Gudrun had brought coin from her house). There, in the warmth of the hearth, they ate smoked salmon. Despite the hot flames, it could not remove the chill from Kai's bones.

The innkeeper sat down next to them on an adjacent chair. "Coldest summer I've ever seen," he said. "What brings you to the uplands in this weather?"

Kai nodded. "We came to make a petition with the king."

"The king is dead, you know," the innkeeper said. "You're from out of town, aren't you?"

Gudrun's lips pursed in concern.

"The king is dead?" Kai asked. "Sigmund is dead? Who has taken his place?"

"Kenna Wildsaber," the innkeeper answered. "She calls herself High Queen. She says everyone in Oskir must take up swords against the southern threat… and she says nothing of the darklings, and the Ulfr threat."

"We humans must unite," Gudrun said. "The Ulfr are a far greater threat than these southern knights… and yet all you Badelgarders care about is ambition. All the while, the crops fail in this eternal winter."

"'You' Badelgarders?" the innkeeper said. "Are you not a Badelgarder?"

"In some ways," Gudrun answered.

The innkeeper frowned. "Whatever you say, lass. Yet if you came to make a petition to Queen Kenna, then you will be disappointed. She allows no lowborns into the Golden House. She has no respect for lowborns."

"I am highborn," Kai said.

The innkeeper spoke in a hushed voice. "I have a feeling she is more vicious than even Sigmund. I would not risk offending Her Grace. If I were a highborn, I would not even ask anything of her."

Fluttering began in Kai's stomach. Perhaps this man was right. "I'm sorry, but it is gravely important."

"What do you want of her?" the innkeeper asked. "I would not risk my life to talk to her."

"I can save Badelgard from the Ulfr," Kai said. "It is up to me,

I'm afraid."

"He speaks truth," said Gudrun. "Tomorrow we must make a petition to her, no matter how dark her heart."

In early morning they arose. The sun had retreated behind silver skies, and flakes of snow drifted down. It struck Kai, as he ascended the stair to The Golden House, how very strange a summer this had been.

Two guards stood there. They crossed their spears, blocking Kai and Gudrun's paths.

"I request audience with the queen," Kai said. "It is of grave importance."

"She does not speak with lowborns," one guard said.

"And she is very busy overseeing the realm," the other added. "Something your small mind cannot understand."

"I am highborn, of the Line of Riverhall," Kai said. "I am of the Order of Scouts; thus my rugged clothing. But I assure you, I am descended from the Seven Wardens, and on equal footing with any other highborns."

"I hope for your sake you are telling the truth," a guard said. "I do hope you know the punishment for lying about ancestry."

"I do," Kai said.

One guard left.

A few minutes later he returned. "Kenna, our honorable queen, tells you to flee Oskir before you are imprisoned. No Riverhalls are allowed," he said. "She has added that one of the members of your baronial house is Alysse, and she is a traitor to the realm. Furthermore, she states that if you do not leave Oskir by tonight, you will be flogged and then thrown from King's Falls."

Gudrun stepped forward, in such an aggressive movement that Kai laid a hand on her shoulder to restrain her. "It is required to stop the

Ulfr," Gudrun snapped. "Everyone in Oskir will die by autumn if she does not hear him out!"

In an instant the shaft of the guard's spear struck her cheek and knocked her down. She fell a few steps. Kai ran down to help her up.

"You have made your request, and your request is denied!" the guard shouted. "Make use of your last few hours. Consider well whether you wish to be dashed upon the rocks of King's Falls."

"What can be done?" Kai said as he and Gudrun walked around low-town. "The queen will not hear us."

"You are the Dragon's-Son," Gudrun said. "You are born to lead, boy. You must bring the Dragon's wrath upon Queen Kenna." Her voice grew loud with emotion. "You must burn her with the fire of your belly."

"Do you mean that I should raid the Golden House?"

"I mean you must lead. I am a creature of the Godly Realm; you are a mortal, and mortals must tend to their own realm. I am here to guide you, boy, and give you counsel. But *you* must lead."

Kai looked down at the cobbled streets and thought silently. He could not force his way through to the Golden House… not without the words of power, of which he only knew one. Perhaps—he reflected—discretion would be his ally.

They left in the early evening. When the bells of the Church of Vana rang seven o'clock, they left the warmth of the inn and entered the cold outside air.

Strange, Kai thought, *that it is cold as late autumn and yet the sun is still out at this time.*

They walked up to high-town, where the wooden palisades blocked entry to the Golden House. More than two guards stood there now; perhaps a dozen in steel mail and spangenhelms had gathered, talking amongst themselves. A hunting party, it looked like, for a fugitive. Perhaps they were looking for Kai.

"We must leave," Kai whispered to Gudrun. "Follow me."

They headed back to central low-town, and before they could exit, it became clear that the two huge wooden doors of the gate were shut, and an iron bar hoisted over them.

Lights caught Kai's eye: a pair of bull's-eye lanterns. The hunting party canvassed the low-town for Kai, the outlaw. They had not given him a chance to leave; apparently they had changed their minds and wanted him dead.

"What will we do now, Dragon's Son?" Gudrun laid a hand on his shoulder. "The Dragon is the leader of our people."

The light of a lantern struck Kai's face. "Steel yourself," he said. "They've caught us. Now, we must let them capture me. Run, Gudrun; they aren't after you. You can come free me."

"It is not for the Daughters of Vana to interfere in mortals' lives," Gudrun said. "I can only give you counsel."

"Then go back to the Godly Realm!" Kai clenched his teeth, stomach churning as rage swelled up in him. "Do not help us. Turn your back on the nation that has worshiped the Goddess for hundreds of years."

Kai stepped forward. A guard shouted, "There he is!"

"What is my crime?" Kai shouted. "Living?"

"The queen wishes you to stand trial," another guard said. "The Line of Riverhall are all traitors."

Despite his surety in what he had to do, Kai gulped, trying to exorcise the trace of fear worming his way up his gut. "Very well. Let me answer to the Queen of Badelgard."

A guard grabbed his arms and restrained him, turned him around and tied some rope around his wrists.

Kai looked into the dark night and saw that Gudrun was gone.

CHAPTER TWENTY-ONE: ALYSSE RIVERHALL

It was dawn when Alysse's army arrived at Oskir. Alysse waited with her mercenaries outside the Golden Gate. The news of Kenna's coronation preceded their coming. The she-wolf had achieved her goal. Yet other news had reached her too. Rumors that Kenna was a witch of dark powers.

In her home country, wizards were allowed to live. Yet a council ruled over them and told all magicians that they must avoid using the power of the Abyss. In such an ignorant, uneducated land, such restrictions would be unheard-of, and wizards would go mad. Alysse already knew Kenna was insane, but her untrained use of magic would explain her dark heart.

The army waited outside the gate, and the guards on the battlements greeted them with jeers. A few ran off, doubtlessly to inform the she-wolf queen.

The mercenaries jeered back, and throughout all their shouts, a uniform chant began: "Hail Lady Alysse! All hail Queen Alysse! *All hail Queen Alysse!*"

Alysse smiled, but it soon vanished when Lady Kenna arrived (she did not wish to call her 'queen'). The she-wolf had a red complexion. She wore black steel mail and held a spear in her hand.

"Damn you, southern whore!" Kenna hissed. Then she threw back her head in laughter.

Mad, indeed.

"Your army is much smaller than I anticipated."

"And where is yours?" Alysse shouted in return.

"I have more than a thousand in my retinue. I outnumber you three to one."

"Just a thousand?" Alysse laughed darkly. "These men by far

outstrip your men in skill."

"You are badly mistaken," Kenna said. "I possess power untold, and will extinguish the southern threat once and for all… I could defeat you even if it were just me."

"Only because of your dark sorcery!" Alysse cried. "Only because you do not fight with honor… you do not fight like a Badelgarder, but instead like an *Ulfr*."

Kenna flexed her hands, as if to work her magic upon Alysse. Alysse ducked, and a trace of cold passed over her.

"Archers!" Alysse cried. "Shoot!"

The bowmen in the back of her army obeyed, drawing arrows to their strings. Alysse watched from her crouching position as several projectiles missed, but at last, one struck Kenna in her mail-covered chest.

She cried sharply and then hurried down the wall. One arrow struck a guard, who was not wearing mail; he fell down from the battlements. His comrades quickly ran off, out of the line of the mercenary archers.

"You gave me an accurate assessment of your skills," Alysse said. "Your men's abilities are beyond compare."

Ivarr—captain of the mercenaries—turned his head from the front of the army and grinned. "Aye. Our boasting is not undeserved, milady… or should I say, Your Grace?"

They waited an hour, and Ivarr and Alysse thought of how they could enter the city without siege weapons. They could craft a battering ram, Ivarr suggested, out of the upland's many trees. Alysse made it clear she did not want to starve the city; the people, in their suffering, would resent Alysse's rule. And she did not want them to suffer, anyway.

As snow swirled down from the silver skies, Alysse ordered a soldier to go chop the wood for the battering ram.

The soldier had not taken ten steps before the huge gates of Oskir opened, revealing an army of Blackhelm axmen ten men wide and innumerable rows long.

"Shields!" Ivarr shouted.

The soldiers in front pulled thick shields over their bodies and drew their spears, forming a wall of wood and steel. Yet the Blackhelm axmen charged them, roaring like bears.

Alysse whimpered softly as she watched. She did not like battle, especially when her life depended on it. But the risk was worth it for the High Throne; it was worth it to save Badelgard, and to honor blessed Harald's name.

A horn peal echoed over the rock-strewn, pine-covered hills of the uplands.

Perhaps it is Sir Logrin and his army, Alysse thought, and the warmth of hope flushed through her. A Zarube knight would not kill a lady... only a she-wolf like Kenna would.

The soldiers fought on, and it seemed that the mercenaries made inroads. The Blackhelm warriors swung their two-handed battleaxes in heavy strokes, and shattered many shields; and yet—having no shields of their own—they were easy prey for the mercenaries' spears.

Archers gathered on the wall. Wildsabers, if their yellow-white swan surcoats were any evidence. Immediately the mercenaries in the back pulled out bows of their own, and the two sides exchanged arrows; several mercenaries died, and one Wildsaber archer immediately fell.

Just a bit longer, and perhaps—perhaps—*Logrin will save us.*

The horn pealed again. It was closer this time.

The fighting continued. The Wildsaber archers made inroads. A mercenary fell every minute from their well-aimed arrows. Yet on the ground, the Blackhelm axmen fared poorly.

"Traitors!" one jeered. "You used to serve King Sigmund!"

"King Sigmund is dead!" Captain Ivarr growled back through gritted teeth. "And you serve a demon, if the rumor is right!"

Soon the thinning mercenary host breached the gate, and only a hundred Blackhelm soldiers remained. Stepping on the piles of bodies, the mercenaries—now half-strength at less than two hundred men—fought an uncertain battle.

At last the horn blew again, and the coming army was within sight. Yet it did not appear to be of Zarube origin. A standard—a skull wreathed in cold blue flame, set against a black field—emerged above the trees.

Ulfr.

Alysse screamed, "Charge!" and the army obeyed. They rushed the Blackhelm axmen who—expecting the mercenaries to keep fighting in their calm, straightforward manner—panicked at the sight of their frenzy.

Within a few minutes, the Blackhelms had either fallen to the mercenaries' spears or fled away. The Wildsaber archers continued to loose their arrows, picking the soldiers off one at a time.

"Shut the gates!" Alysse cried. "We must unite! The Ulfr are coming! *The Ulfr are coming!*"

But the Wildsabers did not listen. They kept loosing arrows down into the host.

"Ivarr!" Alysse said, "Shut the gates! Everyone else, get rid of the archers."

A few mercenaries struggled to push the gate shut. Some others locked it with an iron bar while the rest charged up the wooden stairs to the battlements—a group on each side of the Wildsabers—and then pressed them, cutting them down like swine to the slaughter. At last, the battle was won, and at what a great cost.

But the Ulfr were coming.

CHAPTER TWENTY-TWO: KAI RIVERHALL

The jailer gave Kai a bowl of pottage for breakfast, but he didn't trust it. It could be poisoned. It could be fouled. Instead, he splashed it on the jail's flagstone floor. He wanted to throw the hot liquid on the jailer's scarred, ruddy face.

Gudrun will never come for me, he thought. *She says she is of the Godly Realm. And I am a mere mortal.*

Kai needed to find the lexicon. It was in the Royal Library along with the annals and historical books. It was not a large library like those of other nations; the southlanders called the Badelgards ignorant because of the lack of literacy. Yet Kai could read... a little, at least. If the lexicon were in human script, he could sound out the words fairly well.

Yet, as the ruddy-faced jailer approached him with bared teeth, and laid his meaty hands around the iron bars, Kai doubted he would even get the chance to search for the lexicon. "Your trial approaches. Queen Kenna will decide your fate. But I hear she ain't happy with you, not even a little bit."

Kai stayed silent for a while, calculating his words properly. "I can save Badelgard from the Ulfr, sir. If she would have an audience with me, I could explain to her how to help the realm."

The jailer's eyes looked into his, shallow and thoughtless in the way that idiots' eyes are. "The queen won't hear of it. She ain't happy wi' the Riverhalls."

An idiot, Kai thought to himself. *Perhaps he wouldn't be too difficult to fool.*

"Sir," he began, "How would you like to be a housecarl?"

"A housecarl? Me?" the jailer said.

"I could make you a housecarl." Kai put on a feeble smile. "I am heir to the House of Riverhall... I could make you highborn!"

"A highborn, y'say." The jailer's eyes brightened, and his lips widened into a smile. "Me? A highborn?"

It's working. "Yes, I can make you a highborn. You could live in Andarr's Port with me. You only have to do one thing."

"What?"

"Free me."

The man's smile grew larger, and then suddenly he frowned, his brows furrowed, and he snarled. "You must think I'm a right idiot. I ain't surprised, 'cause people think I am an idiot. But that'll get you a few lashes. And I'll make your execution *really* hurt." He snarled again.

Perhaps, Kai reflected, it is time to use a Word of Power. Perhaps if he killed him, got the key-ring from him...

No. I must be resourceful. I cannot let it go to waste. I may need it later.

Kai clutched his knees as he shivered. Outside, through his cell window, snow had begun to drift down.

A horn echoed in the distance. It sounded like a war-horn of some kind. Who could it be?

He tried to peek outside the window, but couldn't reach it. He jumped, but only caught sight of a silvery sky and infinite snowflakes.

A few minutes passed. The war-horn sounded again. The clanking of iron footsteps echoed. He turned around and it became apparent that Queen Kenna walked toward him, clad in black steel mail that made her appear serpentine, and wearing the gem-studded High Crown. She glared at Kai, brown eyes burning, mouth twitching as she looked upon him. Half an arrow-shaft emerged from her mail, near her shoulder.

"It is time for you to die, boy," she sneered. "All the Riverhalls must be killed... beginning with you and ending with Alysse."

A man ran up to her. "Milady!" he shouted. "Alysse is inside the city! She breached the gate! An army of Ulfr has just arrived!"

"The Ulfr are our friends," Kenna growled. "I have made an alliance with them."

"Surely not, my queen!" the man breathed.

Kai's blood simmered inside him.

Kenna turned to the jailer, eyes blazing. "Do not question me! I am your queen."

"No one who uses the Ulfr to cement her rule is a queen of mine!"

Kenna threw her hands forward. The guard made choking noises and turned red. His veins protruded from his skin, growing bulky with blood. A few of them burst. The jailer cried out, but it was quickly suppressed; and then, a loud pop sounded from his head, his eyes rolled and he fell limp.

Kenna turned around to face Kai. "I have total power over your blood. There is no greater power than blood magic!"

She threw her hands forward. A pressure built up in Kai. His veins bulged. He couldn't speak. He tried to shout. He kicked the iron bars.

"There is a greater magic! The magic of words! *Miuru!*"

Kenna struck the wall. Her body shuddered and bent. Her shoulder popped, and if it hadn't broken, it had been injured. Kai finally had some luck, he thought, until Queen Kenna rose up onto her feet pointed her non-wounded right hand toward him.

"It is as the Great Witch said," Kenna hissed. "You are the Dragon. You stole Cani's power, you dog!"

"You speak like one of the Ulfr!" Kai shouted. "You are a traitor to the humans… you've betrayed your own people!"

"I speak not like an Ulfr! I serve not the Great Witch." Kenna grew tall, head reaching the ceiling as her skin reddened. Sparks of flame burned in her eyes. Her nails blackened. When she spoke again, her voice was low and gravelly, and resounding across the room. "I serve not the Great Mother, but Baa'oul Eater-of-the-Damned."

"So you serve a demon!" Kai cried. "A true demon…"

"The Great Slug hungers." She leapt over to the cell bars in the blink of an eye, wrapped her black-nailed fingers around the bars, twisted and pulled and opened a wide space.

She took a step inside and Kai dove for the opening in an attempt to escape. But she grabbed his calf with a hot hand, and cast him to the floor. She opened her jaw. "*I hunger…*"

Kai struggled against her but she had an animal strength. As her grip tightened, Kai's bones ached. They were breaking.

"Traitor!" Kai howled. His leg bone gave in with a pop. The pain filled him, and he cried out.

His arms tingled, and heat surged through his veins. Gooseflesh ripped across his skin, and his neck-hairs stood on end. Something was changing inside him.

"The Dragon is a receptacle of power!" a female voice thundered from beyond the cell, and it was not Kenna.

A power danced on his fingertips. Not only was he a wizard of words, but also of blood. Kai thrust his hands forward and focused his anger on Kenna.

The scent of lofty mountain meadows reached him. He briefly stopped his magic-working, and looked back. Towering above them, and girt in the winged helmet and golden cuirass of the valkyrie battle-maidens, was Gudrun.

CHAPTER TWENTY-THREE: ALYSSE RIVERHALL

Alysse rubbed her arms in the chill air. Her army had half its original number. Less than a hundred and fifty soldiers remained alive, and the Ulfr host lurked outside the city walls with their blue skull banners. The war-horn pealed again.

"They are coming... the risen Ulfr!" Alysse looked back, and watching with only minimal relief as the mercenaries shoved an iron bar over the gate.

"It is not an Ulfr horn," said Captain Ivarr. "Ulfr horns are low in tone."

Alysse had thought all war-horns were the same. "Their standard is the skull in cold flame against a black field."

"They either stole the horn from a human, or..." Captain Ivarr looked down. "I don't know what else."

"Go check and see."

"I will not risk the arrows."

"Then I will do it." Alysse grabbed her dress and ran toward the wall, then ascended the stairs to the battlements. She squinted as she looked on the fields north of Oskir. Three standards rose above a mass of about a hundred soldiers. On the flag were blue-flamed skulls on a black field. Yet—as the hundred-strong mass drew closer—it became evident that human footmen carried them, and blond-haired Sir Logrin rode on his white charger at the vanguard.

Alysse waited there, standing in the cold air as her breath turned to fog. She had nothing to fear from Logrin. A Zarube knight would not strike down a woman; nothing could breach the code of chivalry more flagrantly.

In time, the army arrived at the gate. Impaled on Logrin's spear was the head of an Ulfr. Alysse could not see it well from such a height, but it appeared to be Cani Orion. Logrin's once fresh and immaculate face seemed weary, and a frown had fallen over his features. "Let us in, milady!" he cried out. "I promise to serve you forever. I have fought the strange wild-men of this land, and have won at a great price. But this I promise you: I will serve you if you will have me. I will be your champion."

"If you have changed your mind about me," Alysse shouted, "then I shall change my mind about you! Open the gates!"

The army passed through the gate, riding and walking.

Logrin hopped off his white charger and his long golden hair flowed across his back. He drew his sword—his long steel sword of Zarube make—and knelt before Alysse. "Milady," he said, "I will be your liege under one condition."

"What is this, Sir Logrin?" Alysse proffered her hand, and he took it in his and kissed it.

Logrin stood up. "I will be made king, and you shall be my wife," he said. "However, you shall give me leave to betray our love. I shall be the worst husband who ever lived; and I shall be given full power over the nation and over you—life or death. You will be queen only in the sense that I am your husband."

The cries of a villager briefly cushioned Alysse against the shock: "The She-Wolf Queen is dead! The She-Wolf Queen is dead! Thank the gods; the she-wolf is dead!"

The news was little consolation. "Milord," Alysse said, turning her head to Logrin. "Do you know anything of chivalry? The Knights of Marabelle…"

"I do not give respect to a woman that deserves none."

"I deserve respect!" Alysse's eyes welled with tears. "Ivarr."

The words had barely left her lips before Ivarr ran forward with his spear. He thrust out the steel head, but—in two strokes—Logrin smote the shaft asunder and, twirling around, beheaded him.

Alysse cried out. A tear streaked down her cheek. "Alas for me!" She laid a hand over her heart. Logrin was a master of the blade, and the footmen and lesser knights that served under him were formidable. "I will marry you, Logrin."

Logrin smiled, flashing his white, powder-bleached teeth. "Come with me, my queen. We shall march to the High King's Throne, and to our conjugal bed."

They ascended the steps together, up past Earls' Court where her husband Harald had stayed with her before his death. The Golden House towered above the city on a high hill. At last they entered, and found that all was in disarray.

The body of Queen Kenna lay on the floor, appearing as if she had burst. A trail of blood followed her where she had been dragged into the throne. Together, Alysse and Logrin and the soldiers walked up to her corpse. Alysse spat upon it.

"Never was a death more deserved," Alysse said.

"Shut your mouth," Logrin snapped. "You shall not speak unless I permit it."

"I will not be treated like this!" Alysse snapped in return. "You are a knight, and I am a lady... a duke's daughter!"

Alysse felt Logrin's metal-lined slap before she saw it. Her cheekbones flared, and tears of pain formed in her eyes. "You truly know nothing of chivalry," she gasped.

Logrin laughed. "Look at where you are, and where I am. I would not insult me, or I shall strike you again and again." He walked up to the throne. "Now I am king. Alysse, bring me her crown and set it upon my head."

Alysse picked the crown from Kenna's bloodied head. Crimson stained the velvet and traces of red ran along the gold. The former High Queen had burst, with huge bloody holes pocking her corpse. It was either wizardry or devilry, and that meant the danger remained in the palace somewhere.

Sitting on the throne, Logrin made his first pronouncements. "I hereby form the House Vis Logrin! In giving command and in inspiring fear, my House shall have no equal. A grinning skull against a black field shall be my coat of arms…"

"Like the Ulfr," Alysse said, slowing her pace toward him.

"So it shall be," Logrin said. "They seem to have something the humans of Badelgard don't: Respectability."

"They also have evil thought and mind."

"'Evil' is what the weak call strength." Logrin smiled again. "It is no matter. I do not care for the Ulfr; must I remind you that I defeated their general? I only like the colors and contours of their flag, and the idea of the Grinning Skull. Yet I must admit, I do respect the Ulfr more than I respect the people of this backward land."

"Do not speak of my people so," Alysse said. "I am a Badelgarder, and—by gods!—I will die for them." Bursting into tears, she threw the crown to the floor. "I care not whether I am queen. I care not whether you kill me, snake! I care only about the fate of my people."

Logrin stood up and drew his sword. "Defying the House Vis Logrin can only end in death."

"And perhaps it will be yours!" Alysse shouted, and looked back. The soldiers and lesser knights of Zarubain stood there in glittering mail. With them, some of the Badelgarder mercenaries looked at her in noticeably duller clothing.

One cried out and tossed Alysse his spear; she caught it. Immediately the two sides charged into each other.

It matters not whether I am High Queen, Alysse thought. I care only about the people.

CHAPTER TWENTY-FOUR: KAI RIVERHALL

The door to the library lay before him, and Gudrun stood behind him in the gear of a battle-maiden.

"The Ulfr lexicon awaits you." The valkyrie put a hand on his shoulder. As she did, shouting and clashing steel erupted from the throne room a few yards away. "The humans selfishly battle for the High Throne. But your concern is nobler. Your goal is to defeat the Ulfr, not to have a shroud of gold on your head."

"I have no aspirations to be noble, but I cannot help but respect a valkyrie's counsel." Kai tried the door. It was locked, as he expected.

He kicked hard. The door shuddered, but the blow hurt Kai's toe most of all. He kicked with the sole of his foot, and the door shuddered again. He kicked once more, harder this time, and a loud *crack!* echoed across the corridor. He kicked again and the hinges whined under duress.

One more kick, and the door gave in halfway. Kai could see the insides of the room now: a dark, wooden-walled chamber barely ten feet wide and twelve feet long. He leapt upon the diagonal door, and with a splintering snap the door fell inward.

Kai could not see the names of the books, only make out vague, square shapes piled along the shelves.

"I must get a torch," he growled.

"No," Gudrun said. She stepped in, and spread her hand; in her palm a luminous orb appeared. "A gift of Vana, to light your path."

"I thought you would never interfere in mortal affairs," Kai said.

"Such a minor incursion would not bother the Council of Gods."

Kai smiled. He searched the room. The books here varied in shape and make: rolled-up parchment scrolls; thick, dusty codices bound in wood; even ancient tablets etched with runes. Kai searched through them furiously. There were books of science and medicine, ancient annals, and—written mostly on the stone tablets—prayers for good hunting and pleas to the gods.

"This will take a while to search." Kai turned to Gudrun and frowned. "I am not a good reader."

"But you are a reader, and that is a rare gift in this land. Now make haste, and find it as fast as you are able."

CHAPTER TWENTY-FIVE: ALYSSE RIVERHALL

The mercenaries—most of whom wore leather jerkins, and only a few of which wore steel mail—soon fell to the longswords of the Zarubes. Sir Logrin looked upon Alysse in his victory, and laughed.

She stood there, holding her spear to her chest as her heart raced. The head of Cani—the Ulfr sorcerer—lay propped against the wall beside the throne. His wild, bearded face seemed to have changed. His eyes were all white, like some hairy wild-man gone mad, and his tongue lolled from his mouth.

"Tell me, Alysse Riverhall," Logrin said, stepping toward her, "what it is your heart desires." His shield—painted with the silver-belled horse goddess—seemed to have darkened to a grey bruise-like color. "Tell me, what it is, my lady fair, that you seek after."

Alysse choked with tears as she talked. "I wish for things to return to how they were... for Badelgard to be at peace again. For Sven Oster to sit on the throne. For my husband, Harald, to lay by my side. For you to be back in Zarubain, where you belong. For things to be as they were, before this fell winter..."

"Alas for you," Logrin said, "for the lady who died at the hands of Sir Logrin; the first victim of his tyrannical rule. The beginning of a series of deaths so numerous that the whole of Badelgard will dwindle..."

Alysse's tears streamed. "And it will be as it was," she said grimly, "and the Ulfr shall return; and it will be all your fault. Nay; it shall be all my fault, because I brought you here. So you shall get your wish. I will not die happy... I will die without Harald, and without honor."

"Your name shall be forever scorned." Logrin smiled. "If there are any Badelgarders to remember your name, they will hate it. If there aren't any, the Ulfr shall consider you a hero."

Cackling, the knight charged forward; the head of Cani emitted a low groan; and Alysse thrust her spear forward.

CHAPTER TWENTY-SIX: KAI RIVERHALL

At last the book was in his hands: a codex with black wooden pages. Kai opened it. The dry, yellow pages were cracked at the edges. Yet Kai could read the black-ink letters.

Bulla: Fire.

Kagan: Winds.

Amon: Heal.

They did not seem to be arranged in any particular order. With the book in hand, Kai left the library and headed toward the throne room. He caught the mountain-pine scent of Gudrun behind him right before he reached the open doorway.

"Do not interfere in the battle for the throne. You must let the ambitious fight amongst themselves. It is not yours to interfere with the petty squabbles... you are the Dragon's Son."

Kai hesitated. Gudrun had the wisdom of the Godly Realm.

Then there was a loud snap of a broken spear, and a woman's shriek. It was shrill and desperate; the final cry of a person who neared death: a choked, panicked scream.

Kai would ignore Gudrun's pleas. He was the Dragon's Son, but he could not hear that shriek and do nothing. He ran in, and saw Alysse Riverhall lying on the floor. Though she was pale and weary-faced, and a bloody wound ripped across her chest, her lips were firm with resolve.

Her long hair was fine and golden as it ever had been; and only a monster would slay a woman like her.

CHAPTER TWENTY-SEVEN: ALYSSE RIVERHALL

A boy stood there. He had kind eyes. He looked like Harald, she thought, as the blood—the *life*—left her. She smiled.

"Do not smile!" Logrin demanded, red-faced. "Remember your place! You will go down in history as a traitor."

Tears fell from her eyes, and mixed with the blood, but her smile remained.

"Stop smiling!" Logrin shouted again.

The boy stepped in. He had a book in his young hands. Yes, he looked like Harald; black hair, dark eyes, though Alysse could not see well through the blur of her tears. Despite her smile, she choked on the salty water. A dribble fell from her wet nose.

"*Bulla!*" the boy shouted.

Alysse wondered what language the boy spoke in. She giggled. Then Logrin caught on fire, and ran around as he burned. She giggled again. He deserved it, she thought. Yes, he deserved it.

The blood collecting around her was warm, and it was spreading. The blood was so hot, and she felt so deliriously warm; it felt good after the wintry summer. Slowly her eyesight began to fade. As she drew in her last breaths, she took in the piney scent of mountains.

She opened her eyes, and looked skyward; and she saw a warm sun, and blue skies, and a mountainous meadow. And she saw Harald's beautiful dark eyes looking toward her, and his lips pink with life. A warmth flooded through her as they kissed; the warmth of unrequited love made real.

CHAPTER TWENTY-EIGHT: KAI RIVERHALL

In the rush of battle, Kai did not notice the last gasps of Alysse Riverhall. He heard the screaming of the long-haired knight, and saw the panicked looks of the lesser soldiers, and felt the restraining hand of Gudrun. But it was only before he shouted "Kagan!" and the winds roared through the Golden House—blowing everything around in a self-contained storm—that he noticed the beautiful woman's chest had stilled.

In a panic—as the winds blew the hot fire this way and that, and the expensive purple curtains caught flame—Kai grabbed her and, with taxing effort, heaved her over her shoulder. As the foreign knights and soldiers scrambled out of the doomed Golden House, Kai followed them. Gudrun was a step behind.

Kai would never forget the sight of the burning of the Golden House. A landmark that had stood for hundreds of years now was gone. Then a clattering and a cry resounded across King's Hill. Kai looked to his right and saw a spear with Cani Orion's head rolling down the steps.

Kai set Alysse down, gently, and rushed over to the impaling spear. He grabbed it by the shaft. Seeing the whites of the Ulfr wizard's eyes sickened him. "Snake!" he hissed, sensing that Cani's power remained beyond death. "You brought this to fall upon Alysse Riverhall. You were responsible, I am sure?"

The pupils and irises returned to his eyes. He glared at Kai. "The Dragon returns…"

"To defeat the Ulfr completely, and with finality."

"You will not defeat Enara, the Great Witch…" His eyes rolled back into his head; once again white, he began muttering. Black ichor dripped from his mouth, trickling through his thick, wild beard.

Kai opened up the lexicon.

"*Laiu!*" cried Cani.

The lexicon went flying; the binding broke and the pages flitted this way and that.

"*Bulla!*"

The pages burned to nothing.

"*Laiu!*" Kai returned, not knowing what the word meant. But Cani's head went flying against the burning wall of the Golden House, and a loud crack of his rented skull echoed across the hillside.

"*Shioru!*" Cani cried.

Kai's entire body shuddered and—for a brief second—his fingers seemed to vanish. The word must have meant 'disappear.'

"That, I assume, is your worst spell!" Kai shouted. "But you have only made me stronger! *Shioru!*"

The copied words escaped his lips and—as the head burst to blood and infinitesimal shards of bone—all that was left of him vanished to nothing.

Kai stooped over and caught his breath. Yet despite his exhaustion, his limbs quivered with anger.

Lady Alysse—desire of every scout in Woodhome—lay still on the hillside, as noble in death as she was in life.

"Oh, to bring her back to life," Kai said. "Oh, to set her up as queen."

"The High Throne is of *no concern to you.*" Gudrun's voice was biting. "I said it before, and I shall say it again; we must leave them be. Come with me, and we shall leave Oskir together, Dragon's Son."

Kai turned to her and glared. "*No.*" His hands shook as he beheld the fully girt battle-maiden. He turned to the hundred soldiers further down the hill, staring at him with wide eyes. "She must be avenged."

He threw his arms and called up the blood-magic. He forced the blood up and down their bodies. He built pressure in all their veins. A stream of blood popped out of one, then another. They screamed but Kai had no plans to show mercy. As he viewed them explode in blood— one by one—his anger only grew. He wanted everyone who had committed the deed dead. He wanted every Ulfr dead, and everyone who helped kill honorable Alysse.

At last every soldier lay in piles of blood. The red liquid flowed down the steps like a waterfall toward Earls' Court. The heat of the burning Golden House hung thick in the air. It staved off the Ulfr fell-winter.

Then he recalled the Ulfr word from the lexicon: *Amon*—heal. "Amon!" he cried. Alysse's wounds sealed, and she took in a gasping breath of air. Relief surged through Kai.

"A hope is borne on the wings of the Dragon," Gudrun said. "To the forest of the damned you must fly… To the place of darkness you must bring Fire and Salt."

Kai's body shuddered. Something was trying to get out of him. It was like an animal trapped inside his back yearned to be free, tearing through his flesh. Throes of pain filled him in sudden bursts. He retched, and cried out. *"What are you doing to me?"* he hissed.

"I am doing nothing," Gudrun said. "The Dragon is in the West; but he has blessed you. Hope is borne on his wings…"

"Hope…" Another burst, ripping through his spine. Even a woman's childbirth could not match this pain, or so it seemed. He cried out again.

One of the Golden House's supports fell in, crumbling, and the palace leaned to the left. Soon it would all be gone. All of it…

The pain reached a climax. Something was tearing through his skin. He screamed, and screamed again. He fell on his face, then staggered forward. With each burst, his back bent. At last, a pair of scaly green wings burst from his skin. He ran forward and leapt off the hill, and his feet did not touch the ground.

"Hope is borne on Dragon's wings!" Gudrun cried out. She ran forward and leapt upon him as he flew. She thrust her spear toward the bright sky. "The Green Dragon has returned, and his fire shall consume all who fight against him! Avast, Ulfr, for the Green Dragon will scorch you with his flame!"

As the wings carried him away, Kai knew beyond doubt that he was the Dragon, destined to fight the Ulfr and bring upon their end.

Book Three, Dragon's Son, is available now.

GLOSSARY

A note on dates: All dates are reckoned by the Imperial system. In 1 Y.E. (Year of the Empire) the first brick of Peregoth was laid, while Y.B.E. (Year Before the Empire) marks dates prior to that event.

A note on Zarube names:
Vis = "Of" in the familial sense, especially when prefacing the name of a noble house.
Diu = Indicates a son or daughter.

Altgard: See *Hall of the Slain*.

Baa'oul: A demon prince known for his gluttony. Known as the Eater of the Damned.

Buntringer: The ancestor of the Badelgard people. His sons were Hjarta, Himnall, and Helgur, from whom the human population of Badelgard descends.

Dragonmount, the: A tall peak in the northeast of Badelgard where the Green Dragon once slumbered. The ancient Ulfr believed it was haunted and knew that a great beast slept there, but dared not disturb it.

Garrone: A small county in Zarubain ruled by the House Sargonnais.

Great Witch, the: The highest Ulfr title, representing the pinnacle of magical power.

Green Dragon, the: The dragon, named Skruga, who allied with the Badelgard humans and destroyed the ancient Ulfr with fire. He is believed to be the last dragon to leave for the west.

Green Dragons: The priesthood of Skruga residing in a stone temple at the base of the Dragonmount.

Hall of the Slain: Also known as Altgard, this is the place where Vana, goddess of victory, and her valkyries are supposed to reside. It is believed to be a spacious longhouse in a mountain meadow within the broader realm of heaven. Only skilled warriors and men of great honor are chosen to live in the presence of Lady Vana and her warrior-maidens. By day, the risen dead fight, but at night, they recover from any wounds they received during the day and feast until the early hours of the morning in the presence of the valkyries.

Healing House, the: The most highly respected center of healing and medicine in Badelgard. Located in Trowfell Keep, the large complex contains steam baths, a vast collection of imported herbs and assorted herbal remedies, and a small library of medicinal texts. A large staff of healers and physicians—associated with the religious order of Vana—attends to the sick and injured.

Housecarl: An order of protectors for the various noble houses. Housecarls are considered highborn and are required to defend their lieges to the death if need be. Appointment to housecarl is the only way a lowborn can enter the nobility. A housecarl can be stripped of his rank easily; all it requires is the liege-lord's verbal pronouncement. The order is open to both men and women.

King's Drawbridge, the: An enormous wooden drawbridge that can only be lowered via the High King's command. It is the only way, excluding sea travel, that a person can enter the low-lying southern lands. In winter, it is Badelgard's sole exit. High King Sven has not lowered it since the beginning of his reign.

Marabelle: The goddess of horses. Called Eliane in Badelgard.

Marabelle, Knights of: A Zarube knightly order and cult, serving the House of Voraigne.

Nobility: The nobility of Badelgard is called highborn and expected to rule above the common, or lowborn. At heart they are a warrior class, and in their inception expected to protect the kingdom and shy away from any temptations of luxury or excess. The top tier of the nobility consists of the earls, who rule great towns and citadels across Badelgard. Below earls are the barons. Only one baronial family owns land and rules its own city: the Riverhalls of Andarr's Port. The other barons rule petty villages. The Osters, an earl family, took the High Throne after the Accession Crisis of 656 and changed the name of the capital from Rigthorp to Oskir.

Skruga: See *Green Dragon.*

Sky Cliffs, the: A sheer precipice separating Badelgard from the low-lying southern lands. They stretch approximately 2,000 feet and can only be descended via the King's Drawbridge.

Somergard: The land of the House Summerleaf.

Sorelden: See Ulfr.

Summerleaf, House of: A Badelgard highborn family.

Troll: A large, hulking creation of Ulfr wizards.

Ulfr: A human term for the people that originally inhabited Badelgard. The Ulfr called themselves the Sorelden, and called their land Sorelda. As a people, the Ulfr had many customs that the human invaders thought to be odd or even evil. They suffered the effects of severe inbreeding due to widespread brother-sister marriages, which caused a number of physical deformities: instead of five toes, most Sorelden had two large toes; only three fingers and a thumb on each hand; and yellow eyes. They worshiped a deity called The Great Mother whom the invading humans identified as a demon. Each year, there was a lottery and those Ulfr families who were picked had to sacrifice one of their children to The Great Mother. Despite their deformities, the Ulfr were powerful wizards and most of them—perhaps because of their worship of the death-loving Great Mother—had the gift of necromancy. With their sorcery, they created trolls: hulking beasts which served them in war. Although the Ulfr were intelligent, rigid adherence to tradition created a refusal to innovate. Hiding on a steely peak was what the Ulfr called The Slumbering Beast—a green-scaled dragon—who soon allied with the invading humans and rained fire down upon their cities and temples. The Sorelden were all gone circa 300 Y.E., not to be seen again for five hundred years... until the current Ulfr Crisis (circa 825 Y.E.).

Valkyries: The warrior-maidens who serve Vana and scour Badelgard for worthy additions to the Hall of the Slain. They are portrayed as beautiful, winged women holding spears.

Vana: The goddess of victory and the home. She is portrayed in art as a big-boned, brown-haired woman in a white robe, often plucking her trademark instrument, the harp. She is the original patron goddess of the Badelgard humans; the other deity whom they worship, the Green Dragon, was added to the pantheon after the conquest.

Voraigne, House of: One of the most ancient noble houses of Zarubain. It controls a duchy of the same name located very close to the royal estate. The Voraignes are one of the kingdom's most highly-respected families.

Waterwood, the:

Woodhome: A hunting lodge and general base of operations for the Riverhall Order of Scouts.

White Wolves: A species of Great Wolves with snow-white coats, pink eyes, and viciously territorial tendencies. In winter, they can often be seen rolling in the snow or bounding through the mountains in a never-ending hunt. White Wolf Keep, residence of the Silverback noble family, is named after them.

Zarubad: A city of about 200,000 people. The capital of Zarubain.

Zarubain: A nation south of Badelgard.

ABOUT THE AUTHOR

Cursed at birth with a wild imagination, Andrew Cooper spent his youth dreaming of worlds more exciting than Earth.

He is a graduate of the Odyssey Writing Workshop. His stories have appeared in Morpheus Tales, Fear and Trembling, Residential Aliens and Mindflights, among others.

CONTACT THE AUTHOR

Visit **www.aj-cooper.com** to sign up for the newsletter and stay up-to-date on new releases.

Find him on Facebook at:

www.facebook.com/AJCooperauthor

DRAGON'S SON PREVIEW

Part One:
My Brother the Morguis

CHAPTER ONE

Thorsten—or Huge Thorsten, as the small people of lowland Badelgard called him—had never seen anything like it. Nor had he, at any point in his life, thought he might. The Golden House, home of the High Kings of Badelgard, burning in a towering inferno. A column of smoke rose up high into the sky, easily visible from where Thorsten stood.

Perhaps it was even more disturbing from his vantage point: outside the door of the low-town inn. Now the lowborns, long poorly-treated, could see for themselves the unmaking of the king and his nobles. The outsiders—the foreigners who entered the city—had freed them from their shackles. But were they better off? Food was in scarce supply. The crops had, in all likelihood, failed. Soon starvation would set in.

Thorsten shivered at the thought.

The sight of the burning Golden House awakened in him something he had tried, in recent days, to suppress. For most of his adult life, Thorsten's lust of gold had ruled him. He had given no heed to the sanctity of life; he cared only about accumulating wealth, and the lives he had ended were without count.

But he had atoned. The goddess herself had come to him in a dream. He had thought himself beyond morality or compassion, beyond help… but one look in the eyes of the goddess, pure and holy, and the weight of his crimes fell upon his shoulders like a mountain. He had gone to Vanaheim, to the goddess's holy temple, and offered all the wealth he could to her—all the gold he had not spent on whores and mead. The goddess had forgiven him, but Thorsten knew someone who would not.

Thorsten's mother lived in Adal Vale. By all accounts, she was alive. Who knew how such a saint had given birth to such unfortunate twins—Gunstein and Thorsten, both thieves and murderers of the lowest degree. Was it her husband? That was anyone's guess. But Thorsten's mother, though close in flesh, could not be further from Thorsten or Gunstein in spirit. Pious to the last, making offerings every week to the gods—at least, from what Thorsten remembered of his childhood. She would never accept him.

And yet, did he have a choice? Winter was coming, and it promised to be the harshest in history. Who knew what had happened to Gunstein? In all likelihood, he was dead: food for worms. And no one would know or sing of him; no one would care. Thorsten and Gunstein, after a falling-out over gold, had split up. And Thorsten could only envision death in his brother's future. It was the price one paid for the kind of life they led.

But regardless, Thorsten had to go to Adal Vale before starvation set in. The evil that had entered Badelgard would not climb so high into the upper mountains; it had not in ancient times, and it would not again. Even if starvation touched the lowland, the valemen were hunters, not farmers. And no matter how cold it grew, no matter how deep the chill, the hunter's bow could always find its mark. Venison and bear meat, trout and mutton from highland goats—those would remain. The greatest question for Thorsten, the one that meant everything to him, was whether his mother would forgive him for the way he led his life.

But he had to go. The burning of the Golden House—the bright flame and the column of dark-gray smoke—showed that the old Badelgard was coming to an end. He would have to go back to Adal Vale. Everything he had was gone; in the high mountain passes rested his only hope.

He had to go now.

He had to prepare for what would be a long journey. Market stalls, set up in the middle of low-town, offered the last scrapings of road-biscuits. The shopkeeper had long abandoned his post, in all likelihood due to the commotion at the Golden House. Thorsten took a handful—perhaps more than was warranted—and tossed it in his sack. But as a gesture of his changed persona, he left the remainder of his money there on the desk: a dented silver penny, and two farthings. All that was left of his life of crime, wasted on years of whores and drunkenness.

A tear fell as he heaved the sack over his shoulders. Past the streets of low-town, beyond the frantic screaming that rose above the crackling flame, Huge Thorsten walked out of the Golden Gate and into the snowy lands beyond.

The wooden markers rose above the snow, showing the path to Huge Thorsten. The day was fading; the sun, pale and weak, grew ever lower in the sky. Thorsten felt the worm of unease wriggling in his stomach. Something was out there, in the pines clustered along the path. He sensed that the world had changed. The trees no longer seemed alive, and the air was a lifeless miasma. Yet beyond this lack of life, beyond the shadows between the pines, something—moving, yet not living— lurked, and hunted.

In time, the darkness was complete. Thorsten ate a carefully-measured meal of road bread, and prepared his bedroll. There would be no tent; he had one purpose, to get to Adal Vale, and comfort was the least of his concerns. Yet here, at nightfall, there was nothing to protect him from the looming darkness, and often he opened his eyes after sensing something was stirring.

Experience taught him that trying to sleep never worked; the Lady of Dreams had to come to you, by her own accord. The best course of action was to relax. Yet pressure mounted in Thorsten, and he wanted nothing more than the pure light of dawn.

As he lay there, eyes shut, a sound—quiet at first—distinguished itself against the constant moan of the wind. A chittering, like teeth, as if someone were caught ill-prepared in the blizzard.

Thorsten opened his eyes. Through a veil of light snowfall, he made out a silhouette. It was a man's shape, heavy-set and tall. It was not one of the small lowland Badelgarders, nor was it as hulking and huge as a troll. It was Thorsten's size, tall and powerfully-built, like one of the valemen.

Thorsten's axe lay right next to him. He reached for it, grasped the familiar wooden haft, and as it did the silhouette responded in kind, darting toward him.

Thorsten scurried backward, out of the protection of the bedroll and into the snow. He stumbled to his feet, and there, in the moonlight, he laid eyes on his brother.

There was Gunstein—Huge Gunstein, as some called him. He did not look well. He was bald, as normal, but his beard—though present—had turned from black to a bronze color. A closer inspection, as Gunstein stepped awkwardly towards him, revealed that his fingernails had grown abnormally long. Thorsten had never considered Gunstein to have exemplary hygiene, but any sane person would trim nails of that length.

"Brother," Thorsten said, "you do not look well." A heady stench hung about his brother.

Gunstein spoke. "Thorsten." His voice was higher than he remembered, but memory is a cloudy looking-glass. Yellow teeth protruded far beyond his dark gums. "I am so glad to see you."

"You do not seem yourself, brother," Thorsten said, "but indeed I am glad to see you. Gladder than I've ever been to see anyone." And it was true. Thorsten's friends were few by any measure. Now, his own flesh and blood was here, right before him... but he was not the same. He touched Gunstein's hand, and it was cold. Something wasn't right with him. It seemed impossible that a living hand could be that cold. Could he be one of *them* that the rumors spread about? The dead who walked? It did not matter. Living or living dead, his brother was before him.

Thorsten embraced Gunstein. His brother's entire body was

cold. The sickening smell for a second overwhelmed him, and he stepped back.

"Where are you going?" Gunstein said. "This road leads into the mountains. You aren't going back to the Vale, are you?"

"I was…" Thorsten read disapproval in Gunstein's oddly sallow eyes.

"You don't really think mother will forgive you, do you?" Gunstein laughed. "She would never forgive us. She is pious to a fault, thinking only of what is in heaven rather than what is on earth."

Thorsten wasn't sure if he agreed with the characterization.

"She would not let you into her house," Gunstein said. "She would send you out in the cold and let you die. Don't expect forgiveness. You have committed crimes she cannot forgive."

"I would not speak of our mother that way," Thorsten said.

"You must come with me." Gunstein's grin was strangely wide, despite his flaccid, drooping skin. "We are still friends. I will be your companion. But do not fool yourself; our mother will never forgive us for the lives we've led."

"Gunstein." As he observed the loose skin, noticing a slight greenish hue despite the lack of light, the transformation of his brother fully dawned on him. "What has happened to you? You are changed."

"A man slew me months ago," Gunstein said. "A swordsman of great skill, a scion of a noble house. Well-trained, well-equipped, and well-born like we never were. He landed a killing blow, but he did not escape with his life."

"You are dead, then. But you talk. How is that possible?"

"Days later I awoke," Gunstein said. "I was surprised at first. I stretched out my fingers… they were strangely numb, but I could move them. I took my first steps. I realized I was more powerful than I ever have been. My meager spirit was replaced with a great intelligence. I realized I could live a life superior to my former self. All Badelgard is at my fingertips… and yours, too, if you will accompany me… brother."

"I… I don't know… Mother—"

"Silence!" Gunstein hissed. "I told you, mother would never

have you back. She despises us both. In her mind, we are vagabonds. She would never forgive us. So stop suggesting it."

Thorsten looked down. "I…" He could offer no argument. A weight fell over his heart. If only he had made better decisions. Thorsten and Gunstein—devil-children—killing their stepfather, an upstanding valeman. The few who lived there chased them out, and so they descended into the lowland to live a life of crime. Who could forgive Thorsten? After what they had done, any hatred toward Thorsten was more than deserved, and any love was unwarranted.

He looked down into the quickly-accumulating snow. If Thorsten had done things differently, perhaps it wouldn't have ended like this: the dead of Badelgard refusing to rest in their graves, a dark pall spreading over all things, and a winter that promised to last a lifetime.

"Where shall we go?" Thorsten's voice was quieter and hoarser than he intended.

"Since mother will not accept us," Thorsten said, "I know a place… the few good men in Badelgard left, they are making a last stand. They've hoarded food all summer and autumn. They have enough to last through the winter. I wanted to tell you, my brother, because you are my flesh and blood."

"And how did you find me?" Thorsten wasn't sure he wanted to know the answer.

"In my new state I have powers of great intelligence, but also scent."

His entire manner of speech had changed.

"In my past life you and I were blood-brothers," Gunstein said. "Do you remember our pact?"

Age fourteen. Two cuts. Hand-and-hand. A promise that they would never do harm to each other; and a vow that they would spill the blood of any who harmed the other. Of course, they spilled the blood of many more, and in time even the bond itself was broken. "I remember," Thorsten said.

"Then as blood-brothers, we must go," Thorsten said. "At dawn, follow me. I know you humans need rest."

CHAPTER TWO

When the sun's first rays glanced through the trees, waking Thorsten from his rest, Gunstein stood in the exact same position he had left him. And now, in the brightness of the morning, Thorsten realized how cadaverous his brother looked. To say he did not look well would be inaccurate; he looked dead, and his skin had a sickly green tint. His yellow eyes were soupy. Flies buzzed around him. But he was Thorsten's brother.

He is my brother.

"Are you ready?" Gunstein said.

"I am," Thorsten answered, and at once set about packing his things.

Thorsten guessed they were somewhere in the nebulous border between Trowheim and Ostergard. The snow had accumulated over the night, and now reached the ankle. The sky, for once, was blue and mostly cloudless. But the chill had deepened so much that even in his bearskin cloak, his thick winter cap, and his multiple layers, numbness began to spread through Thorsten's body.

Gunstein was ill-prepared compared to his brother. He wore a light summer kirtle, inappropriate for the harsh weather. The faded green wool was torn in places, the telltale rips where evil wounds had fallen. Despite the lack of clothing, Gunstein did not shiver. Perhaps it was one of the gifts of living death.

"Let us go," Gunstein said.

Thorsten gave one passing glance to the glorious peaks of the Dragonteeth—jagged purple rock half-covered in a sea of green pines—and gave up the hopes of his journey there.

Thorsten followed his brother through a pine thicket. The snow seemed even deeper here, though it was likely just an effect of the thick black boughs.

"What is it like to be dead?" Thorsten said as he pressed through the wall of trees.

"What is it like?" Gunstein's voice had changed in his new state; it was higher, shriller, now. "To live beyond death is the greatest gift of all. It is on the level of godliness. I am a higher being. I am beyond the cares of the mortal world: beyond pain; beyond hunger and lust; beyond the shackles of morality. I wish you could be like me, brother. Maybe you will be, one day."

"I don't want to be," Thorsten answered. "I am happy that you are happy. But I don't want to live beyond death. One life is enough for me. One life of mistakes… one life of murder and theft. I do not want to live again."

"Perhaps you will have no choice," Gunstein said.

Thorsten gulped. He didn't know why his brother had said that. It did not matter. He had to remember that his own brother was with him now; flesh of his flesh, bound together in a blood-pact. He walked with the only person in this world who would forgive him for his crimes, who would call him "friend." They shared entries on the Hangman's List on multiple occasions; and each time, managed to collect enough gold to bribe their way off it. Yes, this bond of brotherhood could never be shaken.

A clearing opened up before them. Gunstein ducked behind some bushes. "Get down!" he hissed.

Thorsten took cover behind the trunk of a spruce. His confusion lasted only a few moments before he realized his brother's purpose. Footsteps echoed through the wintry morning air. Many footsteps.

Out of the veil of the trees something finally emerged. He was perhaps seven feet tall. Black full-plate armor obscured every part of his body. Spikes protruded from the pauldrons, and the images of tortured, groaning faces were painted on the dark steel. From within the giant greathelm, two red eyes peered out like ghostly lights. Rime covered his gauntlets. He wielded a giant sword in both hands, and its blade—a pale white color—glowed with cold. Around this dark warrior, an air of wintry gloom radiated, chilling not just Thorsten's body but also his soul.

Behind this dark champion, a group of underlings marched. There were a dozen in immediate view, but doubtlessly more behind. They were humanoid. If elves, the most twisted and perverted of their race: heavy-set and tall; their chests and faces so hairy they appeared bestial; thick, disheveled beards of copper and brown; and pale yellow eyes.

From the right of the clearing, another group emerged to meet them: a dozen humans. Sons and daughters of Badelgard that had defected, perhaps. Thorsten had no respect for cowards.

"My lord Arani," said a Badelgard man, girt in the chain shirt and hand-axe of a warrior. He knelt.

"Slave." The champion's voice was many-threaded, like a choir. "I have summoned you to this meeting for a purpose. A morguis has broken free of Lady Inana's control. You humans are too weak to dispose of a morguis, but if you find it you will tell us. We cannot have an insurrection of the living dead. They were created by our wizards. They are slaves like you, even if they are far more useful. Do you understand?"

"Yes!" the Badelgard man shouted. "Yes, my lord. I will do whatever I can, as always. Long live the Great Witch and her supreme goddess."

"The morguis is the paramount achievement of necromancy," the champion said. "No other civilization has discovered the means of making them. Despite their vast power, they have a weakness: intelligence. If you find the morguis, inform me at once. If you do not, I shall dispose of you in the most painful way possible. Your torture will last years."

"Yes! Yes!" the Badelgard man cried. "Long live the Great Witch and her supreme goddess!"

The champion turned around. The dark army departed. The humans turned and went their own way. Thorsten remained silent and unmoving; Gunstein waited several minutes before his brother stood up and motioned for him to do the same.

As he stood up, waves of nausea coursed through Thorsten. "What in Varda was that?"

Gunstein's yellow eyes widened. "The man in armor is one of the Sorelden."

"Sorelden?"

"You humans call them Ulfr."

You are human, too. Thorsten shivered.

"His black war-plate means he is a Fell Lord. A tiny handful of Sorelden males survive the necromantic transformation. Those that do are girt in the dark armor, and given rime-frost blades. A wound from a Fell Lord's sword cannot be mended except by the healing masters of Danarion…"

How much my brother has changed, Thorsten reflected. He and his brother were as uneducated as they came. Where and what Danarion was, he had no idea, but it sounded Elvish. In life, Gunstein would never know such things. Of the two brothers, Thorsten had been considered the smartest; yet in a crowd of lowland Badelgarders he was always the least intelligent.

The conversation between the Ulfr lord and the human slaves did nothing to ease him. What had they spoken of? A "morguis"… some kind of twisted Ulfr creation. It had broken free of its controls. It was dangerous. It was the most powerful of the undead.

As he looked into his brother's soupy yellow eyes, long-devoid of life, a chill settled over him. *Is my brother the morguis?*

CHAPTER THREE

What was a morguis? Why was it dangerous? Undead were walking corpses… how could they differ in strength? If his brother was, indeed, the morguis, were his words of affection insincere? Was he luring Thorsten to his death?

The chief question remained: What was a morguis? As he struggled through the windblown snow, Thorsten began to wonder if he should turn back while he had the chance. Mother would never forgive him; Gunstein, morguis or no, had convinced him of that. He did not deserve forgiveness. But perhaps Adal Vale would be a good place to retire, to let the forces of justice bring about his end. He was a valeman in a world of halflings, and perhaps he should die as one. At the very least, he could tell his mother how she had been right all along; he had made poor decisions and ruined himself, and she could say, "I told you so."

"Where is this hideout?" Thorsten said. "Who is there, and how do you know about it?"

Gunstein halted his lumbering steps and turned around. His eyes narrowed. "Don't ask questions, brother. Trust me in my new form; I am wise, and know the proper paths to take."

"What if I want to know?" Thorsten snapped. He laid a hand on his axe haft.

"Do not touch that weapon!" A shrill screech, completely unlike his brother and, perhaps, not altogether human.

"What is our mother's name?" Thorsten would not be daunted.

"What?" Gunstein's eyes narrowed further. "Why do you ask this?"

"I want to know if you're really my brother, or if you are someone using my brother's body."

Gunstein bared his teeth. They protruded far beyond his black gums. "Our mother is Gerta. Our father—rest his soul—is Bjarn son of Adalf. Do you have any more questions, brother?"

"What was our dog's name?"

"Aron," Gunstein hissed. "Big, even for a mountain dog. You rode him when you were little… fell off every time. Satisfied?"

The memory brought a half-grin to Thorsten's lips, but it vanished instantly. "All right. I'm satisfied, brother."

But in truth, he was not.

Gunstein turned and, together, they continued their journey through the thick stands of spruce, the frozen streams and the drifts of snow. Each step was reluctant. Still, he clung to the hope that his brother's soul remained inside him; yet this hope, tenuous already, faded fast.

CHAPTER FOUR

They did not cease their march until night fell. In darkness, a heavy snow began. Thorsten ate the last of the road-bread. He set his bedroll out. Gunstein stood and watched.

"I will make a fire," Thorsten said.

"I hate fire."

"You *what?*" Telling Thorsten not to bother wouldn't rouse any suspicion, but stating it in those terms was downright strange.

"Don't make one," Gunstein said. "That's final."

"Am I your brother or your slave?"

Gunstein snarled. "I would not risk my anger."

"Again. Am I your brother or your slave?"

Gunstein roared and ran at him. Thorsten clambered to his feet and readied his axe. Before he could pitch it back, Gunstein struck him across the jaw with such force that he toppled over into the snow.

Before he could reach for the axe his brother was on top of him, pinning his arms into the snow, filling Thorsten's nostrils with his fetid stench. "I said not to risk my anger. It was a warning. Next time, I won't hold back."

Thorsten bit back a caustic reply. This was not his brother. His brother Gunstein was violent when roused, a burglar and a vagabond. But he would never threaten Thorsten.

"Don't even think of escaping in the night," Gunstein hissed. "I can follow scents for miles off. Your brother was stupid but I am not."

"And who are you?"

The monster spit in Thorsten's face. The moisture was thick, adhesive, and smelled fouler than a thousand rotting corpses. "You will come with me. You will not ask questions; it is beneath me to answer them. To answer your question: no, you are not my brother. You are my slave, my catch, my game, and I shall do what I like with you. Try to resist me, and you will regret your decision."

In the monster's yellow eyes, Thorsten glimpsed a different person, a new intelligence: primitive yet cunning, remorseless and predatory, superhuman yet grossly subhuman. Waves of revulsion pulsed through Thorsten's body; he flipped over and vomited into the snow.

Was this the morguis that they spoke of? It did not matter. Whatever intelligence had overtaken his brother, it posed incredible danger to Thorsten. Escaping would take more wit than a lumbering valeman would ever possess. Thorsten was not the equal of this undead monster, morguis or otherwise.

Thorsten wept into his bedroll. Eventually sleep took him.

The morning light illuminated a new reality. Things looked much the same: thick snow, spruces and pines, and wilderness all around. But "Gunstein"—not having slept at any point in the night—stared at Thorsten as he woke from his slumber. Unmoving as a statue, yellow eyes open wide and reflecting no human emotion. Thorsten would have to fight this monster, morguis or no, but he had to use caution. He had no doubt that the creature's threats were not idle; it would not give Thorsten an easy death.

He could only stare in those sallow eyes for a fleeting second. Quickly he looked down and at once set about packing his things. Then he stowed his axe across his back. Surprisingly "Gunstein" made no quarrel, but perhaps this creature was confident in its power. It made sense—if this were the deadly creation called the morguis—that it had nothing to fear from a steel axe-bit splitting its head.

Thorsten moved slowly and reluctantly through the snow, covered in gooseflesh and nauseous. Where was this creature taking him? Certainly not to any safe haven, as it initially promised. If it was the escaped morguis, then it would not take him to its Ulfr creators either. If it wanted to devour Thorsten, then why hadn't it acted by now?

It was a mystery he did not want to ponder.

As the march went on, it became evident they were headed

north. Likely they were somewhere in Trowheim, and Blackhelm Keep, therefore, was not far-off. But trouble had fallen upon Badelgard. The Ulfr—risen from the dead by some black spell—walked freely among the humans. Thorsten doubted the Earl of Trowheim had any power to save him. Their nation was doomed to an eternal winter and a mustering of the restless dead.

Onward they went. The false Gunstein marched fast, taking unnaturally long strides. When Thorsten fell behind, the monster threatened to bind him with a collar and tie him to a leash. The more Thorsten thought about it, and the more exhausted he became, the better getting dragged across the snow began to sound.

Yet he continued at the hurried pace. At noon, famished and exhausted, Thorsten cried out, "I need to eat!" and fell to his knees.

"There is no food," the false Gunstein said, "and if there were, I would not let you have it. Now get up and keep moving, or I will make you yearn for Hell."

"I already do!" Thorsten growled. He began to reach for his axe but quickly thought better of it. It was not the right time, not the right place.

"Believe me, I can make things much worse on you. You are testing my patience. Get up now!"

Thorsten let out a shrill scream as he obeyed. His legs were jelly, only barely supporting his weight. He staggered on, more sluggishly than ever before. False Gunstein slowed his pace, but it was a matter of practicality; compassion was alien to him, now.

The sun dipped low. The northern mountains appeared, the roof of the world. Jagged purple, capped in snow like their brethren in the east. Thorsten had once loved these peaks. He had once loved many things, but now all he could think about was the hulk lumbering in front of him; his own brother, changed after death and given false life. Seeing

Gunstein's body—green, giving way to rot yet animate—sent more waves of revulsion through him.

Then, as a chill wind blew out of the mountains and sent stinging snow into Thorsten's eyes, the false Gunstein shouted out, "The Ulfr are near! Hurry, brother!"

"I am *not* your brother!" Thorsten again reached for his axe, and again drew back his hand. A question presented itself to him, now: *would I rather the Ulfr kill me, or this soulless mockery of my brother?* It took only seconds before Thorsten decided to slow his stagger, and then to stand still.

Gunstein turned around. His eyes bulged, and though dead and watery, infinite rage burned behind them. "Hurry, or I will make you yearn for Hell!"

"I already do," Thorsten hissed, and—grabbing the wooden haft—readied his axe. It had served him well in battle, and it would serve him well now. Or so he hoped.

Gunstein ran at him. Thorsten dove into the trees just as a group of Ulfr emerged from the trees.

"There it is! The morguis!" The Fell Lord was not with them. A few members of the Ulfr party wore iron caps, but most had little armor. This granted them mobility, Thorsten noted as his false brother's attention diverted to the warriors.

The morguis darted at them with the speed and reflexes of a mountain cat. One Ulfr warrior, unencumbered, dodged out of the way. Another was less lucky; the morguis slammed its shoulder into him. The Ulfr went flying and hit a tree with a back-breaking and trunk-splintering crack.

Just as Thorsten noticed one Ulfr with a bow, an arrow flew at the morguis. It stuck deep into its back, but seemed to do no harm. Thorsten's brother, the morguis, tackled another Ulfr warrior and rent his ribcage with its fist.

A purple tentacle-like thing began to wriggle out of his brother's nose. Whether the sight sent him over the edge or if he quickly thought better of watching the battle, it did not matter; Thorsten turned and took off into the dark woods at a sprint. *Please, gods,* he prayed, *I am not worthy of an answered prayer. But let the Ulfr defeat my brother the morguis.*

Cloud cover and new snowfall quickened the coming night. The air was dead and still as Thorsten sprinted through darkness, fearing no bear or White Wolf, fearing only his brother's dead yellow eyes and the evil that had overtaken his mind. With or without his mother's forgiveness, he should never have accompanied Gunstein. But if he had refused, the morguis would not let its prey go so easily.

As the sky darkened and night closed in, Thorsten's exhaustion caught up with him. His sprint slowed to a jog and then to a stagger. The forced march had drained all his energy. Here he was, in the wilds of Trowheim. A wide swath of land separated him from Oskir; and who knew if it remained a human city? The Ulfr now wandered Badelgard freely, growing in strength by the day. What human warrior could match the strength of a Fell Lord?

Despite his exhaustion, Thorsten kept moving. He could not— he *would* not—be captured by the morguis again. The Ulfr, for all their dark magic and the evil customs that lived on in legend, did not seem as cruel or inhuman as the morguis. And though Thorsten kept up his stagger, he knew that in the darkness behind him, the false Gunstein— fuming at his failure—would resume the hunt as soon as possible.

A chill wind blew out of the west. Snow began to fall. Thorsten guessed it was midnight but there was no way to tell. The moon—seen only in fleeting glimpses among the shifting silver clouds—was full and bright white. In Adal Vale, Thorsten's grandfather had spun tales of men changing into bears by the light of the full moon. What a great gift that would be right now, Thorsten mused. As a valeman, he knew full well that bears were swift, that they could outrun a human and perhaps a morguis. Bears were deadly, but they were noble, and the valemen respected them above all beasts.

The winds tossed the snow into a blinding powder. Thorsten's body grew numb. He continued through it because he would prefer Lady Winter's deadly embrace to ever seeing the morguis again. But more than cold, he was growing exhausted—more exhausted than he had ever been—yet the mental image of the morguis drove him forward harder than a cattle prod.

At some ungodly hour, a distinct noise emerged out of the snow. At first, rustling bushes—and Thorsten at once thought of the morguis—but then bells, and the huffing of a horse. A shrill voice called out something in a language he did not recognize. Thorsten quickened his pace. But soon the vast shape of a horse and its rider overtook him.

For a second, the silvery clouds parted, and the moon spread its light all over the wilderness. A woman rode on the horse: an Ulfr woman, her black hair tied in a bun and her skin strangely hairless in comparison to her male brethren. Her robe was black and silken, with a rigid collar, and embroidered with skulls. Her large yellow eyes focused intensely on Thorsten. Then, after the instant's illumination, the silvery clouds covered up the moon, and she was once again a black shape against the trees.

"Who are you?" she said in the Badelgardic tongue.

"Thorsten son of Bjarn," he replied, and realized he feared her less than his false brother. "Who are you?"

She did not reply. She turned and shouted something in her own tongue.

Then—a harbinger of his presence—gooseflesh covered Thorsten's skin, and heavy iron steps heralded the coming of Arani, the Fell Lord. Against the darkness, the red fires of his eyes appeared. In the same many-stranded choir of voices, he spoke—of all things—in the human tongue: "Killing him would be most unwise, Lady Inana. The morguis has marked him as its prey. We should use him as a lure."

"That is wise," Lady Inana replied. "The morguis is the pinnacle of Sorelden achievement. It is unfortunate they are so proud and intelligent; but it is in the larva's nature."

Larva. A word Thorsten had heard before, yet did not know its meaning.

"I must regain control of the morguis very soon," Lady Inana said. "That much is clear. Left by itself it can wreak great havoc. But in the end, our struggle is minor. The Seat of the Great Mother is nearly out of the ice. Our armies roam freely across the land. We have slaughtered humans in droves. In time, the rebel undead will fall under our sway... with me, or without me."

Arani took a few more heavy iron steps toward his lady. A cold like nothing Thorsten remembered filled him, covered him in gooseflesh and chilled his soul. He wanted nothing more than the fell blade through his heart; but instead, he would be lure to the morguis.

CHAPTER FIVE

If—in the bright light of the morning—the Ulfr were surprised by the morguis' absence, they were not any more surprised than Thorsten. As he struggled to sleep, he had no doubt that his brother the morguis would find him, defeat this party of Ulfr, and drag him to its hellish den. But here he was, alive. The sun shone brightly upon the glittering white snow. The sky was bright blue and nearly cloudless. The day would have seemed hopeful if the Fell Lord Arani did not loom above him: a grim statue of black steel, his white blade pulsing with a cold that pierced the mind.

Thorsten wanted to beg the Fell Lord to slay him. But he doubted that pity ever motivated the Ulfr. Surely, if he pleaded with Arani, the Fell Lord would only wish to prolong his suffering.

Thorsten took in slow, deep breaths. The aura surrounding Arani seemed to deaden the air, and make each inhalation twice more difficult. He sat up from his bedroll, now covered in rime frost. The Ulfr lady Inana had dismounted from her horse. Now, in the light of day, Thorsten could see her fully. Her deep eyes—though yellow—would be the envy of Badelgard woman; her wavy black hair, tied into a bun, somehow reflected nobility. Her staff, made of gnarled dark wood, and topped with a skull-shaped gem, was doubtlessly an implement of magic. She was an Ulfr witch, a necromancer, a disturber of the dead.

"Has the morguis lost the scent?" Arani's red eyes flared brightly and dimmed just as quickly.

"A morguis will never abandon its quarry," said Lady Inana. "To the exclusion of all other things, it focuses on its chosen prey... even though your soldiers' flesh is just as savory for its young, it will not abandon this *Thorsten*."

Feeding its young—a thought Thorsten wished had never crossed his mind. But what were the young of a morguis? Thorsten had a difficult time imagining a litter of false Gunsteins, each yellow-eyed, rotting and green like their parent. No matter how he pictured it, the thought sickened him.

And the thought of being fed to the ungodly litter… gnawed and devoured, slowly.

He retched.

"Perhaps we should go west," Arani suggested. "If we draw close, perhaps he will take in our scent."

"Never underestimate a morguis." Lady Inana ran her fingers along the warped wood of her staff. "It will come for its quarry. It will die to find its quarry. It will find Thorsten's scent in time, and we must be prepared for it. If we journey toward the morguis, we may be caught unawares, and that will spell our end. Capturing the pinnacle creation of Sorelda, and returning it to my control, is no easy task. Preparation is key."

Arani bowed his helmeted head. "Yes, Your Worship."

Lady Inana and Thorsten exchanged glances. How deep, how bright yellow were her eyes. Yet Thorsten saw no life in them, nor any compassion. Keeping him alive was no act of mercy; if they let him die, they would lose their lure. If they lost their lure, they would lose control of the morguis. And once they gained control, who knows what would happen? A stroke from Arani's blade, spilling Thorsten's innards all over the snow? Or would they let the morguis—now under their control— have its quarry, and feed Thorsten to its young?

He retched again.

A few hours passed. Thorsten's stomach growled. He couldn't remember the last time he ate. The road-bread had run out long ago, or so it seemed. He glanced at Inana. The dark lady was looking at him.

"The giant is hungry." Inana pursed her lips. "We must not let him go to waste. But food for the dead is not fit for the living." Her eyes, for a moment, seemed to glow. "Arani, you have a bit of the *honthal amani* left over from your long slumber. It is useless to you now. Let him have it."

"As you wish, milady," Arani said. He removed a small cask from his belt and handed it to Thorsten.

Thorsten took it. No sane person—valeman or Badelgarder—would accept a gift from the Ulfr. But how could it harm him? If they wanted to kill him, they would have done it by now. He unplugged the stopper—made of coarse bone—and drank whatever was inside.

The liquor was harsh, but it filled him with warmth. Within the span of a few moments, his hunger vanished, too. He handed the cask back to Arani. "Thank you."

"It has taken away your hunger," Inana said, "and it has made your scent more powerful to the morguis. In this, we have both received what we desire." She smiled, revealing mangled yellow teeth. Her eyes remained the same as always: bright yellow, beautiful and enchanting, yet without life.

It was late afternoon when things began to stir in the makeshift camp. Thorsten watched as his companions—Arani, the Fell Lord, and his lady-liege—moved from their posts, looking into the forest as an icy gale blew down from the mountains. Powdery snow blinded Thorsten's vision, but a familiar scent of rot reached his nose. In the western sky, silver clouds had begun to roll in, veiling the sun.

Through the black cover of pines and the whirling snow, Thorsten made out a dark shape. Hulking, seven feet tall: a morguis inhabiting the body of Gunstein. Even from this distance, its fetid stench had begun to overwhelm him.

Inana crouched and bent her staff forward, assuming an offensive stance. Lord Arani took several heavy iron strides in front of his lady and drew his white blade. Thorsten grabbed his axe from the ground, where his captors had left it lying. He reminded himself that he was not fighting for the Ulfr; he was fighting for his own survival, and these two champions of darkness were only temporary allies.

The morguis took its first lumbering steps.

Inana shouted something at it.

"I have assumed the body of a human!" The morguis roared his reply. "I will only answer in the human tongue."

"Very well, worm!" Inana shouted. "I am your master because I gave you life. I brought you out of ignorance, out of the mindless morass of vermin-kind. Once you were a maggot, the wicked spawn of a fly. It is I who brought you into intelligence, and it is I who gave you your pride! *Submit to me!*"

The morguis shrieked. "Out of my mind, witch! It does not matter that you created me. I am superior, now, to you and all others who walk on two feet. You must submit to *me*. Now give me my prey, or I will destroy you and your companion."

Inana thrust her staff forward. Wind burst from her, and in its wake, an air of power filled the forest. The morguis shrieked again, shriller than before. "Listen to me, vermin!" Inana screamed. "Listen to me, worm! Surrender to your creator. Surrender to your master. I have given you your strength and your sentience, and I can take it away. Remember that your mother was a fly. Remember that, at heart, you are a maggot!"

Thorsten retched. If she spoke the truth, it was more disgusting than he had ever envisioned. A maggot, given intelligence and life through fell powers... was that a morguis?

It shrieked as it charged toward Lady Inana. Thorsten recognized the struggle about to ensue. He had to make the best of it. In either party's company, he would die. If he—now nourished back to health from Arani's liquor—could run far enough away, perhaps he could find safe haven. Perhaps he would not go to Adal Vale; perhaps he'd go to the southlands, soft as they were, free of the fell winter and the armies of darkness that roamed Badelgard.

He sprinted into the darkness of the pines. Inana continued her shouted exhortations. Even as Thorsten fled the air of her magic, it remained around him for many hundreds of yards.

CHAPTER SIX

The light of the sun dwindled. Thorsten continued his sprint as long as he could sustain it, but not much time passed before he slowed to a stagger. His throat burned and his lungs were taxed to their absolute limit; his legs could barely sustain a walk. Not even the fear of the morguis could drive him any faster. His body wouldn't allow it.

He hacked and coughed, and his throat was so hoarse that breathing in the cold air filled him with pain. As the sun set and darkness flooded in, and the snowfall picked up, he wondered if he should give in. But all he had to do was picture those yellow eyes and he found the energy to continue the stagger.

At last the darkness was complete; a fetid stench filled his nostrils and Thorsten realized he had fallen face-first in the snow. He looked up and saw the half-rotted body of Gunstein. The morguis was here. He vomited.

The hulking giant, mock image of his dear brother Gunstein, hauled Thorsten into its putrid arms. A rotten stench filled Thorsten's nostrils as the morguis spoke: "I've found my prey."

Thorsten, now, had discovered how his life would end: as food for the spawn of the morguis, nibbled and gnawed alive until only bone remained. But it would end; that was enough consolation. Through all the bites and the horrid pains, he would remind himself that it would end. Hell would await him, a fitting punishment for his crimes. But Hell could not possibly be worse than this.

Thorsten fell asleep in the putrid arms. When he awoke, perhaps he would find himself in the morguis' den.

In the red light of dawn, Thorsten realized that the morguis had carried him to the foot of the mountains. With long strides, it ascended a steep incline with its former brother in tow. The peaks, covered in snow, appeared directly above him. In the blood-red sun, he realized his axe remained clipped to his belt. The morguis had nothing to fear from such simple weapons, or so it seemed.

"The Sorelden have lost our trail." Somehow it knew Thorsten was awake. "When we reach my nest, you must not struggle against the younglings. You certainly do not have the power to slay them, but they are weaker than me."

Only an alien mind—one that did not understand human emotions—would make such a suggestion. Perhaps a morguis felt no pain, or did not fear death. The thought sickened him.

Thorsten grabbed his axe, ripped it from his belt. The morguis moved with imperceptible swiftness, swiped the weapon out of Thorsten's hand and cast it onto the snow. It skidded down the mountainside and then was still.

The last hope, gone. The gods had decided: Thorsten would be food for the morguis' younglings. He fell still and determined to struggle no more.

Thorsten awoke as they approached the mouth of a cave. The sounds of shrill hisses and wriggling echoed from within. Thorsten's heart stirred from his slumber; his blood went cold as he drew closer to his doom. He writhed in the morguis' grip, struggling against the iron strength of its hands. At last—whether by chance or his own guile—Thorsten fell headlong into the snow and out of the morguis' grip.

He ran down the mountainside, letting the incline speed him along, but within seconds the same putrid hand gripped his wrist.

"Surrender," the morguis hissed, and dragged him toward the mouth of the cave.

The sun spread its rays only partially into the cave, but that was enough to grant dim light. A few feet in, the stone ground gave way to a precipitous drop. Within the pit, Thorsten caught sight of the monster's young.

Where one of them ended and another began, Thorsten could

not tell. In truth, the thousands and thousands of them formed one wriggling, writhing mass. Individually, they appeared—in some ways—like the maggots one finds in spoiled meat. But a closer inspection revealed mouths full of tiny needle-sharp teeth, and as they wriggled and hissed, it became clear that they were starving.

"My babies," the morguis whispered. "They will fight over you. The strongest one will burrow into you and assume your mind. My child and I… existing in the bodies of two brothers. I can't think of anything that will bring me more joy. I will be united with my child, both in mind and in body. No other morguis is so lucky."

A wave of cold air fled through the cave mouth. The morguis larva in the pit let out a collective shriek, and their wriggling became even more frantic. The sight sickened Thorsten even more and he vomited again.

Arani appeared at the cave mouth. In one hand, he held his white blade. In the other, he held Thorsten's axe. "Your quarry left me a token. Without his guile, I would never have located your den!"

The morguis screamed. It slammed its fist into Thorsten, and he went flying into the pit of vermin.

www.ingramcontent.com/pod-product-compliance
Lightning Source LLC
Chambersburg PA
CBHW020607250626
47154CB00004B/1402

9780615939995